The Doctor's Vision

Fiona McArthur

Chapter 1

As Sophie Sullivan braked, another squat boab tree dropped a leaf at the side of the road, a sure sign the wet season was nearly over. Her fingers pushed the car horn for the frilled-neck lizard basking in the middle of the dirt track. He reared on hind legs, spread his neck frill and hissed, making himself more than he really was.

Typical male. No, not typical. Just like Brad.

At least the craggy red mountains that embraced her were solid and true, she thought, seeking gratitude instead of sadness as she drove towards the boulder-strewn river. That range in front of her was a dear part of home. Home was reliable.

Home: far north Western Australia, the Kimberley, a place blissfully away from the city and a man who shed lies like the boab shed leaves. So, so good to be home.

Even the dusty Gibb River Road looked attractive until she saw the vehicle parked by the Pentecost and the motionless man beside the sluggish water. Auditioning for crocodile fodder. She sighed - travelers caused her no end of concern - especially ones who hovered for long periods at the edge of the crocodile inhabited rivers.

The tourists parked their vehicles beside the river because of the view to the Cockburn Range across the ochre plains. Locals used the designated parking area at the top of the hill well away from the water.

She pulled up next to the expensive all-terrain vehicle and wound down her window. 'You okay there?'

The man didn't answer. He must've heard her truck. She was ten feet away from him.

Finally, he turned his head and glanced at her. Dismissively, as if the weight of the world rode his strong shoulders. 'Fine, thanks.'

He was big – bigger than Smiley who topped six-two – and this guy looked muscle-packed so he'd be a nice solid mouthful for any croc, but he was too close and too stationary in a dangerous spot. It would be a shame to waste that body, she thought. And, with the new knowledge from Mr. Brand-name Brad she could have done without, it would be a waste of the designer jeans and top of the line Garmin watch.

Congratulations were in order for her immunity from the male species. A hard won but valuable lesson. Go her.

Sophie bit back another sigh. How did you tell someone to get back in their vehicle when they blatantly ignored you?

'You've seen the warnings?' She looked at the sign and read it out loud. 'CROCODILES INHABIT THIS AREA. KEEP AWAY FROM THE EDGE.'

But her reading it didn't make him face her. In fact, no further response to her at all.

Despite the 'leave me' flags that waved from the man, she tried one more time. 'About the crocodiles here...'

'Yes, thanks.' This time he shifted his stance so he faced her. 'I'm just passing through.'

'You'll pass right through a croc,' she said dryly. 'I lost my dog in a spot like this.' And still had nightmares about the tragedy her lack of concentration had caused.

Their eyes met. He wasn't to-die-for handsome, really, but he had those dark, dark lashes and an intense grey gaze that held hers, a might too effortlessly, for someone totally immune.

Metallic, bright, intense. It was as if she'd heard a trumpet call. DANGER, and not from crocodiles. Her skin prickled.

'I'm sorry to hear about your pet.' His voice, low and deep.

Their gaze held. Stuck. A flypaper connection.

Suddenly Sophie could hear the lap of the water, the stirring of the leaves in the trees, feel the rays of the sun beat through the windscreen... or she hoped that explained the rushing of warmth under her skin.

Her eyes dropped but didn't leave his face as she concentrated on a small scar on his chin, white and fine, that made him seem less imposing – more vulnerable – which was a funny thing to think about a stranger.

Sophie searched for the question she'd asked.

He dropped the connection as easily as he'd captured her. 'If I get attacked by a croc because I had to talk to you, I'm going to be extremely unhappy.'

Sophie blinked. What the heck was she doing? Leaving was a great idea. 'Right then. Your funeral.'

For the first time in the ten years since her seventeenth birthday, Sophie crunched the gears as she slipped her vehicle into reverse and got herself out of there.

Levi Pearson turned back to contemplate the spot his father had been taken five months ago. Or had he been pushed and the crocodile only secondary to his demise?

He'd find out. Soon. Before he left.

That tiny whiff of suspicion, something only he seemed to have inhaled, was the reason he'd flown up here at the end of the wet season, and why he'd asked his – damnably determined to accompany him - sister, not to mention their connection to Xanadu.

Suspicion and the fact the other consultant he worked with had recommended a holiday for the tenth time in the last two months had put him on the aircraft. His sister, the one he had trouble saying no to, he couldn't shake so she came too.

As soon as he'd confirmed or dismissed the concept of foul play he'd get himself and his sib the hell out of downtown nowheresville and fly back to Sydney. The manager here looked more than capable of running "Xanadu" and Levi didn't need another burden. Problem was, since his arrival he'd uncovered a possible motive for foul play he couldn't dismiss.

He took his eye off the bank and risked a glance at the blonde woman's four-wheel drive vehicle as it ploughed through the river away from him.

Nothing else mattered.

Hadn't for a long while.

Definitely not a pair of concerned blue eyes under two stern eye-brows. Except for a frozen few seconds he hadn't expected when their eyes had held, she'd been officious and determined. But now, not so easily brushed away from his thoughts.

Thankfully, he'd read the population of the Kimberley region sat about thirty thousand people in an area slightly larger than Germany. He should be safe from bumping into her again. He didn't need the complication of drawing attention from a local – or a local drawing his attention when she lived three thousand miles from Sydney.

A stealthy splash to the left pushed his attention firmly back on the water. Levi took a few steps towards the vehicle he'd borrowed from the resort. Probably better not to get eaten and give her the chance to say I told you so.

He could feel the twitch of his lips at the thought along with surprise at the idea of smiling – something he hadn't done much of in the last year or two – and climbed back into his vehicle.

Nearly two hours later Sophie swerved around another pothole and the old Landrover truck bounced off what felt like the thousandth corrugation on her way to Jabiru Town. They'd grade the road soon, now the rain had stopped.

She gritted her teeth to stop the jarring. Almost home. Almost.

Funnily enough, she wasn't tired. Hadn't been since the Pentecost River. She didn't want to think about the man at the river anymore. It had been one of those moments in time when you catch another person's eye and for a second or two (or three), glances tangle and reverberate, and then you both look away – or one of you rolls their eyes - and the moment passes.

Except that particular moment in time seemed to last forever and she was still waiting for it to pass.

An instant. A man. A stranger. With dark eyes. A great body. And a hot mouth.

Even in the scowl she remembered, his mouth had hinted at a fullness and dangerous curve that made her wonder how he'd got the scar. Maybe some hot-blooded woman had thrown a plate at him. Her lips twitched but she pulled them back into line.

He'd looked everything she didn't want in a man.

City, yes.

Rash, definitely.

Stupid for not heeding the sign...

She frowned. He hadn't looked stupid; actually he'd looked fearsomely intelligent. So not stupid, maybe reckless.

She didn't want that either. No way. She didn't want any of him.

Worst of all he'd had the trappings of Brad. Though more discreetly, classily wealthy than her flamboyant ex, Dr Bradley Gale. The man who had promised to love her and honor her – she'd thought he meant only her, until one of his other true loves was having a baby.

She was finished with people who thought they could buy you. Serve you a prenup with the engagement ring. And sleep around.

She was glad to be home in a place where people said what they meant and meant what they said. Where she could be useful to those who needed her, and not only as some decorative arm hanging, and thank goodness not confined to answer when spoken to.

What had she been thinking?

She drove through her tiny town – mostly boarded buildings except for the pub – to their house, a modest timber residence with bull-nosed verandas on all sides and a tiny dry garden. Neat and comfortable, in the same state as they'd inherited it from their parents, who'd inherited it from their parents after granddad lost everything else.

A place where Smiley could save every cent for his dream station like the one his grandfather had been tricked out of in a card game all those years ago. Against a rich man who'd lied. A man like Brad.

Not that Smiley lusted after Xanadu, which had crippled their own father with loss. Smiley had his own plans for a different station, hence the reason his cattle were agisted all over the Kimberley while he saved for new land. But Smiley didn't complain. He achieved. Silently.

Sophie did wonder if Smiley had become used to his bachelor ways while she'd been away. He'd looked surprised when she'd moved back into her old room, even if 'Fastest engagement in history,' was all he'd said.

She could hear him moving on the front veranda.

'You must've loaded the cattle early. I didn't see the road train on the way in,' she said as she rounded the veranda, then stopped. He had someone with him. A pregnant someone. A very pregnant someone.

'Ah, you're here. My sister, Sophie.' Her brother indicated the petite dark-haired woman beside him. 'This is Odette. From Sydney. She's in the area for a week or so and wanted to meet a midwife in case she had any questions.'

Her brother's drawl had slowed, which was saying something, as his normal speech defined the word unhurried.

Sophie smiled and nodded at the vision. Beautifully dressed. Perfect hair and make-up. Interesting, as the heat usually melted foundation around here.

And she recognized her watch. Cartier. Brad had bought her one just like it.

She'd left it in Perth.

Sophie bit back the thought. She'd become judgmental and that wasn't like her... or hadn't been before she'd tripped off to Perth for her midwifery and managed to fall besotted and blindly into love. She needed to get her new prejudice under control. Wealthy tourists kept a lot of people in jobs around here and this woman might need her in an emergency.

'Nice to meet you, Odette. Welcome to Jabiru Town. Sorry I wasn't here earlier.'

'I flew in an hour ago.' Her coral-colored lips tilted as she smiled. She had a sweet face, Sophie thought, and warmth shone from her eyes.

'Guess I should have rung first,' a miniscule shrug, 'but I thought the clinic was open.'

Sophie looked across the street to the old shop that had been turned into the clinic. 'I've been visiting an Indigenous Community north of here. It's "women's health" day. Takes a few hours to cover the distance.'

'So Smiley was explaining.' She looked shyly up at Sophie's brother.

Goofily, Smiley actually "smiled" back, an occurrence so rare it derived his nickname. She'd never seen him look like that. Or be much into explaining anything, let alone with strangers. She'd be lucky to get a dozen words out of him on a normal morning.

'Odette flew herself in the chopper,' he said.

Impressive. 'You're a pilot? Wow.' And very pregnant, but she didn't say it. Too obvious to state.

Odette shrugged with a smile. 'I do it for fun. You're a midwife. Wow.'

Sophie had to laugh. 'I do that for fun, too. My friend, Kate – the other midwife – flies her own plane from Jabiru Homestead, so some of us fly.'

Odette had an excited friendliness about her that made Sophie smile. 'So, you're having a baby. And want a check-up? Would you like to come across to the clinic now?'

Odette turned sparkling eyes to Sophie's brother. 'Thanks, Smiley. I hope I get to see you again.'

He nodded and tipped his hat.

The two women crossed the road and Odette cast a quick look over her shoulder. 'Your brother's a handsome man.'

Sophie blinked. She'd never thought about it. He was just... Smiley. 'I don't often see his face. If he's not in the house, he's got an Akubra on.' But she'd look next time. 'I guess I still see skinned knees and freckles.'

'I didn't see any of those.' Odette sounded almost dreamy and Sophie grimaced. City women and remote range Smiley did not fit together at all. Her brother had been so single-minded he hadn't even had a local girlfriend that Sophie knew of. He'd be even more naive of flirtation than she'd been.

'Is it your husband's helicopter?' Not very subtle.

'I don't have a husband.' Odette met Sophie's eyes without a flicker. 'The father of my baby is dead.'

Bummer, for more reasons than one, Sophie thought. Was she being judgmental again? 'Sorry for being nosey.'

'That's okay. Better to get it out in the open anyway. I found out too late he wasn't a nice man.'

I hear you there, Sophie thought. 'I'm sorry,' she said again, because she didn't know what else to say.

'And the chopper belongs to the resort where I'm staying.'

'That would be Xanadu, then.'

It wasn't a question. Xanadu. Now an ultra high-end resort a hundred kilometers away, as the chopper flew, catered for a Kimberley adventure with five-star luxury. Private suites, fine wine and cuisine, and escorted tours with private sittings in the hot springs and gorges. They'd turned it into a wilderness park with a few token cattle. Not like in Grandfather's day. 'I've never known them to lend the chopper before.'

Odette shrugged. 'I just asked the manager.' She looked across at Sophie. 'I could take you and Smiley up for a fly if you'd like.'

'Thanks, but I'm a ground dweller.' She smiled. 'Should you be flying when you're pregnant?'

Odette pushed her hair from her eyes. Rolled them a little. 'You sound like my brother.'

Now why did she suddenly think of the man at the river. 'Don't suppose he's a big bloke, scar on his chin, not into smiling?' The one who was "just passing through."

'That's Levi.'

'Levi?' Well, his jeans did fit nicely.' Now she was being silly. Because it seemed he was another person who was happy to bend the truth, as opposed to the people from around here who didn't lie.

'That's his name. And yes to your ever-so-accurate description.'

'Then I guess I have met him. He was at the Pentecost River crossing.' Sophie didn't say a little too close to the water, because she didn't want to worry Odette. She shrugged. 'I warned him about the crocodiles.'

Odette pursed her lips for a moment then visibly pushed whatever had caused the look away. 'He knows about the crocodiles. But thank you. Levi is a good guy, he's just forgotten how to have fun.'

Sophie needed to talk about something else because she had the feeling anything else she learnt about him wouldn't help her forget.

'When's your baby due, Odette?'

'A month.'

Sophie fought to keep her jaw from dropping but she had another look. Surely too small. Maybe Odette had it all tucked away. 'I'd say your brother was right and you shouldn't be flying.'

'Lucky he's not hearing this, he always thinks he's right. Classic big brother who acts as my parents.'

'Where are your parents?'

'My mother died when I was a baby.'

Oops, Sophie thought. Another foot in mouth question.

Luckily Odette didn't seem worried. 'Levi brought me up. Our father ran off with another woman just after I was born. That's why Levi's serious. He's been the man of the house for a lot of years.'

Too much information. Postives about a man she didn't want to like. Not hearing this.

Sophie pushed open the door and they went into the small exam room. She gestured to the chair beside her desk. 'Have a seat.' Sophie crossed to the sink against the wall and washed her hands. Could have done with a long cold drink but running the cool water over wrists would do for now.

When her hands were dry she settled at the old desk next to Odette and woke the computer. Opened a new screen.

'If it's okay with you, I'll scan your antenatal card and transcribe the main bits into here. Then if you have any worries, I can talk you through most of it on the phone.'

Odette grinned. 'This is like booking into a spare hospital.'

No. It was not. 'I'll check your blood pressure, feel your tummy and have a listen to your baby's heart rate.' Sophie smiled back. 'But we don't have babies here for birth.'

Odette settled herself and held out her arm. 'That's okay. We'll probably be back in Sydney in a few days anyway.'

Maybe that does justify as passing through and he didn't technically lie. Though what the heck was he doing bringing someone this pregnant way out here, so far away from home?

Sophie wrapped the cuff around Odette's arm and the next few seconds passed while she listened and checked. She unhooked the stethoscope from her ears and smiled. 'Blood pressure's perfect. One ten on sixty.' She indicated the footstool beside the examination table. 'If you can climb up there we'll see where this baby of yours is hiding.'

Odette chuckled. 'Everyone says I'm small but I was only five pounds when I was born. The ultrasound said it's a boy.'

Sophie draped a thin sheet over the lower half of Odette's body and Odette lifted her shirt. 'A boy. Wow. Nice tummy.' Sophie was serious. Odette's abdomen curved up in a perfect small hill, brown and smooth, and the baby shifted a body part into a small point as Sophie laughed. 'Look, he's waving.'

Odette slid her hand over the point and the baby subsided as if trained. 'My baby's no sloth. Moves heaps, especially at night.'

'Women tend to feel their babies at night when they're not busy like they are in the daytime. They say the baby already has a rhythm so if he or she's awake a lot at night you might be in for some sleep deprivation.'

'I don't mind.' Odette smiled dreamily. 'I can't wait.'

Yes, you can wait, Sophie thought, as she measured the mound of Odette's belly. Taking into account the petite mother, the measurements confirmed Odette's estimated due date. She slid the hand-held Doppler over the area she'd palpated as the baby's shoulder and the sound of the baby's heart rate filled the room. They both listened and their eyes met in mutual acknowledgement of the wonder of pregnancy.

'There you go,' Sophie said, as she turned off the Doppler. 'One hundred and forty beats a minute and just as perfect as his mother.' She helped Odette sit up. 'Everything looks great.'

'Thanks, Sophie. I feel better just talking to you.' Odette climbed down and smoothed her clothes. 'How much do I owe you?'

Sophie shook her head. 'Free service. Anyone can walk in and get the same. When I'm here.'

'You and Smiley should come over to Xanadu on the weekend. You could have dinner with my brother and me. Our treat. As a thank you for this.' She gestured to the examination couch. 'I'd come and get you in the chopper. Or Levi could.'

Lord no. And she thought they were going in a day or two? It was only Monday. She walked her to the door. 'Thanks, Odette, but the weather's still too unsettled for me. I'm a chicken in the air. I don't know what Smiley's planned. I've only just moved back from Perth.'

'Sure. I'll ring later in the week.' Odette stopped and turned back with a new idea. 'If you're not keen on flying, you could stay overnight and drive back the next day. In fact, that sounds more fun anyway.'

Sophie felt pushed by a small very determined whirly wind, spun and disorientated like the one that just at that moment lifted leaves outside her window. The pane rattled with dust. No way was she pushing herself onto Odette's tall, brooding brother. 'I'll mention it to Smiley.' Not.

Odette pulled a gold compact and gloss from her bag, flicked open the mirror, and touched up her lipstick. Not something Sophie did regularly out here in the bush, and the thought made her smile to herself.

Odette snapped shut the compact. 'What's your brother's real name?'

Sophie had to think for a moment. 'William.'

Odette nodded as if she liked it. 'I think I'll call him William.'

'It's been a while since anybody has.' Now where was this going? Nowhere, she hoped. 'He may not even remember it.'

'Even more reason to,' Odette said cryptically.

That afternoon, Levi poured his sister a chilled juice and himself a cold beer before he moved to look over the veranda at the gorge below. Then her words sank in. He turned back to her. 'You what?'

'I invited Smiley and Sophie to stay over for a night on the weekend.' She sighed as if he was the tiresome one. 'The midwife and her brother. To have dinner and drive home the next day.'

Unbelievable. She would do his head in. 'Did I mention not drawing attention? Until I find out if anyone around here hated our father enough to push him into that river.'

Odette crossed her arms and leant them over her large tummy. 'Hated him more than you? Is that what you mean?'

Levi shook his head. 'I didn't hate him. I didn't respect him or like him, that's all.'

He fully intended to sign the ownership he'd unexpectedly inherited back over to his sister, another baffling development his estranged father had left for him, when they'd all expected Odette to be willed the resort automatically.

Odette rolled her eyes. 'Because he had another son to another woman and deserted us for them. Humph.' She returned to topic. 'Sophie's only just moved back from Perth and Smiley is—' she paused and her mouth curved, '—just Smiley. He hasn't a mean bone in his body. They wouldn't know anything about Father's accident.'

He flung his hand out towards the view. 'We don't know that. Your new best friends, you've met them, what, once?'

'You've met her too.' Sophie sipped her drink and sat forward as he frowned.

No, he hadn't. Hadn't met anyone. Avoided people. 'When?' He'd done his part.

'She said she'd met you.' Odette poked out her tongue. 'This afternoon by the river.' She sat back satisfied.

By the river. The blonde with the soft mouth. He remembered her instantly because she'd lodged like an annoyingly sharp bindii seed from the grass in his memory bank. 'Blonde pony-tail? Nice, umm, features?' Last person he needed to be exposed to again.

Odette coughed and he couldn't help the curve of his own lips. Unlike Odette, he didn't have socializing on his agenda on this trip. He needed to go home. He'd already been away past his expectations and his theatre list would be a mile long if he kept putting back his return. People needed sight and the list kept growing, which was why he didn't do holidays.

His sister would be the death of him but he couldn't deny her much. Too many years making sure she was safe and happy and loved. Because their father had certainly dropped the ball on all of those. Her boyfriends had nearly done his head in and the last one, he couldn't forgive himself for not protecting Odette from him!

He loosened his shoulders. Too late now. And now she'd invited more people. 'So why can't we fly them in and out? That way they don't have to stay.'

Odette shrugged. 'Sophie doesn't fancy the chopper.'

He thought about that. Some people didn't. 'Maybe she wouldn't mind so much if the pilot didn't look like she was going to break her waters any moment.'

'Don't start again.' Odette flapped her hand at him. 'You're too used to feeling responsible. Let me worry about me.'

Sure. But look what happened the last time he'd done that.

Chapter 2

Five days later.

'I don't know how you talked me into this.' Sophie glared at her brother.

Smiley kept his eyes on the road. 'You've been twitchy all week.'

'And you've been moonstruck like a big old cow.'

Smiley turned to look at her briefly but didn't say anything. It was disappointing. A bit of a spat might have taken her mind off the nerves that were building ridiculously at the thought of meeting the jean mogul again. She was even avoiding his name in her thoughts. How ridiculous.

Unable to get a rise out of Smiley, she turned to watch the scenery flash by. The overhanging escarpment of the Cockburn Ranges in the distance ran along the right side of the vehicle. The stumpy gums and dry grass that covered the plains ran to the left. Past the plains were the ochre red cliffs that later would tinge purple as the sun set. The peace wriggled under her armor of strain and soothed her frayed nerve endings with afternoon beauty.

She blew out a breath and her shoulders relaxed.

Sophie knew the darkening gorges hid pockets of tangled rainforest and deep cold pools. But the stands of thick trees made her smile. She'd missed the pot bellies of the grey trunked boabs the most while she'd been in Perth.

'Why don't you like Odette?' Smiley mulling. So, she had got a rise. Something in his voice warned her not to be flippant. He might even be cross. Not a usual occurrence. Funny how she didn't want a spat now the vista had calmed her.

'Who wouldn't like Odette?' she said carefully. 'She seems lovely. I'd just hate to see you hurt when she flies back to her home in Sydney.' That spelled it out.

Ire steamed off her brother in waves. Say what? Smiley frowned at the road ahead and Sophie winced. More displeasure than she ever saw. So rarely encountered and she didn't like it. 'I'm sorry, Smiley. I have no right to judge your friends. I can't see her as an outback girl or you in the city, so a growing attraction might be painful in the end. But it's none of my business.'

'Thank you.' His voice grated the two words into a statement. Thanking her for agreeing it was none of her business. Crikey.

Since her parents had died, she'd become used to bossing Smiley around, giving her opinion, and he'd never seemed to mind. Easiest guy on the planet. Until now.

She'd crossed the line with Odette. Someone he'd met once. Best button her lip and trust Smiley's instincts.

It would've been easier for her if she'd sent him to Xanadu on his own, though.

She had the feeling her trepidation for Smiley was tied up in the trepidation she held for herself with Odette's mysterious brother. And that was queer too. So, she'd stop dwelling on imagined problems.

Smiley turned off the main dirt road onto the red dust of the track through the scrub. They splashed through several watercourses and wound through the red hills until they turned at the "Private Property, No Entry" sign that hid the homestead.

'Welcoming,' she mumbled, and Smiley glanced at her.

'Odette said you've met the brother.'

'Briefly.' She could be just as reticent. She didn't enlarge and Smiley didn't ask again. Then the homestead came into view.

Xanadu homestead was a long low building, and she'd been too young to remember visiting in her grandparents' day. Apparently now it had been divided up into luxury suites perched on the edge of the escarpment. They hung above the river that flowed beneath it like a ribbon of brown.

The main building faced into the sunset which glowed lilac and promised more. Nice place to holiday if you had the credit card to cover it. She thought of Odette. But not when you were eight months pregnant.

Why would Odette and her brother come here now?

At least the thought gave her something else to concentrate on as they drew up at the house. She wondered what the other guests would think of outsiders being invited to invade their sanctuary. What month was this? April. The resort must have only just opened for the season anyway.

Odette swayed onto the main entrance portico in a muslin caftan that looked cool and elegant and Sophie wondered how she could still be graceful when she was supposed to be awkward in the last month of pregnancy. Judging by Smiley's face he'd just seen the Holy Grail.

Sophie sighed and felt for the handle to climb out of the truck when her door moved away from her grasp.

'Welcome to Xanadu.' The jeans man held out his hand and Sophie wasn't sure if he wanted to shake hers or help her from the vehicle.

Where had he come from? She'd been hoping to see him from a distance, to give her time to get her face straight.

She resisted the urge to snap her hand back to her side. Argh. Forced herself to let him take her fingers.

'Thank you.' Be polite. Polite is good.

Long, strong fingers captured hers as a feeling of ridiculous warmth passed between them at his touch. No, it hadn't. Nothing to see there.

She hadn't felt a thing. So why rub her hand surreptitiously behind her back? And why did he look down at her with one enigmatic eyebrow raised as if he'd been surprised as well.

Then Odette was dancing around the car like a classy puppy as she gazed adoringly up at Smiley. Oh Lord. Smiley grinned back. Smiley didn't have a hope.

Odette said, 'This is my brother, Levi.' Levi left her to shake Smiley's hand. Smiley actually returned the shake. Usually he nodded and kept his distance.

'Now, come and see the place.' Odette stared up at her brother with her beautiful eyes excited. 'It's so good to see you, William.' Odette flashed a smile at Sophie before she captured Smiley's hand and tugged his fingers to make him follow her.

"William" looked back at Sophie who managed a tiny smiling shrug that said she'd be fine.

'My sister can be impetuous,' Levi said grimly.

'My brother can't.' She watched Smiley leap up the stairs after Odette. 'Or I didn't think he could.'

Levi lifted one eyebrow sardonically. 'Welcome to Xanadu. I'll send someone for the bags when we get inside.'

Sophie glanced in the back of the truck. 'Actually, we're used to carrying our own.'

He inclined his head. 'But I'd be offended. Please come in.'

The bags weren't worth fighting over so she turned resolutely towards the entrance. He went on. 'The resort's not technically opened for the season and we have the run of the place.'

'Well, that's very nice.' But she couldn't help thinking, how the heck did you do that? They must know the owners extremely well or have unlimited funds. More of not her business. 'When does it open?'

He glanced at the sky. 'Depends on the weather and the state of the roads, though apparently next week, if all continues well.'

She slanted a look across at him. 'I guess you and Odette will be gone by then.'

Another enigmatic brow lift. 'Trying to get rid of us?'

They crossed the gravel drive to the stairs and she paused. 'You did say you were passing through. A week ago.'

'I lied.' Straight-faced, no remorse. Liar like Brad, then. And she'd been attracted.

Sophie felt the cold wash over her. The full bucket. 'People don't tend to do that up here.'

She'd known he was dangerous. Her instincts had been right. Like sniffing the briny scent before a storm. He was trouble.

She started walking again, faster now, but he kept pace. Beside her as if he sensed some history there. 'Necessity can make liars out of us all.'

She could feel her lip curl. 'Some people say that.'

She felt his gaze on her and no doubt he could see her distaste. She hoped so. 'A man, perhaps?'

'I'll look for my brother.' She turned away but he stepped in front of her and she pulled up short to look up at him with raised eyebrows, actually astounded that he would invade her personal space.

'I assume you're unaware out here we're used to wide open spaces and few neighbors. We don't do space invasion well.'

He stepped back. 'I apologize, Sophie.' To give him his due he looked as perplexed as she felt.

'Thank you.' At least she could breathe. 'Smiley tends to wave at people rather than shake their hands. We're not used to people brushing up against strangers in elevators and on city streets.' The "like you" was unsaid but implied.

His mouth twisted in an apologetic smile. 'We seem to have got off on the wrong foot. Twice.' He lifted a hand as if he had no idea why. 'Why do we rub each other the wrong way, do you think?'

No way was Sophie going there. 'I'm not interested in rubbing against anyone.' That didn't come out right.

His almost-smile turned into a grin. 'Let's go in then.' He gestured with his hand for her to precede him, but he didn't touch her. And she didn't thank him for the courtesy because she could feel his eyes on her back uncomfortably the whole way up the steps. Because he was back in her space.

Levi watched her walk sedately ahead of him and they both knew something had happened. Her silly comment had blown apart his defenses. No rubbing then. He smiled again but then it fell away.

Moments of confusion didn't happen to him. He was a stand-alone guy. Yet he wanted to come up beside her and put his hand on the small of her back, feel her heat, and he curled his fingers into his palm to stop reaching out.

Crazy, top-end insanity because how could she invade his head with the tiny bit he'd seen of her? Yet stepping out of the car today, touching her hand, her skin, inhaling her scent, in full blown presence she raised his awareness like a teen on full moon.

Her dress floated simple and blue but smoothed the slender line of her back and hips as she swayed in front of him. Brown legs were bare and long enough to dream about. There you go again. This was crazy.

It felt as if a wire from one of the fences dragged him along in her wake and there was a tautness he could see in her shoulders that said she wasn't comfortable either.

What was it? Apart from totally impractical and heinously inconv enient... but then again, the travel agent had quoted the Kimberley as a destination for new experiences. Not going to happen.

He ushered her, with great restraint and no contact, through to the veranda where the others were sharing the last of the sunset, or at least her brother and his sister shared it, he and Sophie separately observed. Maybe not even that because he wasn't looking at hills bathed in purple.

Swan's neck. Hers flowed like an orchid to her throat. He'd bet her skin...

He shifted his scrutiny away from temptation. He couldn't see her eyes from where he stood, but he knew they were blue. Like her dress. High cheekbones, snubby nose that should have just been snubby but turned out deliciously cute, and those lips.

He reefed his eyes to the glass on the tall round table. Took a long swallow of the beer waiting for him.

Who was he and what had happened to the normal, sane, over-worked man who'd arrived last week?

'Odette tells me you're a midwife,' he said, and now he could see her eyes. Her pupils were big and dark and he fantasized that was sign of arousal.

She ran her finger around the rim of her glass and even that tiny movement made him swallow. 'And community nurse, and anything else that needs medical attention,' she said.

Maybe he'd get sick. 'Sounds diverse. It must be a heavy workload.' He watched her face light up and leaned back to enjoy.

'I relish it,' she said. 'Love it in fact. I've just finished my midwifery masters so now it has the added dimension of meeting people like Odette who'd benefit from access to a midwife before they transfer to a hospital.'

Passion for her job. Bless her. He used to have that. Now he didn't even want to talk about work. 'Odette said you've just returned from Perth?'

The smile died on her mouth.

He felt it as she chilled. Even her pupils constricted until her eyes were light ice-blue again. She jutted her chin and he regretted the question. Obviously bad choice of conversation and a major setback. Probably a good thing.

'Yes. It's great to be home.' Such a cold, emotionless voice, so different from when she'd spoken of work.

She put her glass down and turned to his sister. 'The view is wonderful, Odette.'

Sophie pretended to be absorbed and tried to fade Levi into the background. She didn't want to think about Perth and the fool she'd made of herself there. Though it served as a reminder not to be foolish here.

Externally, Odette's brother was hard to ignore, but internally he'd already lied and invaded her space like Brad had done when they'd first met.

She could feel him watching. Could feel the brush of his analytical scrutiny as if she were some strange species he hadn't figured out yet.

Made her want to think of some witty–slash-cutting thing to make him back off.

But of course she couldn't think of one. No doubt tonight in bed it would be there on her tongue. While she tossed and turned.

She straightened her shoulders. Refused to squirm. Offered her own inspection. He'd be used to city women falling all over him but he'd come to the wrong place for that.

Here a woman wanted a man with more to his repertoire than looking good.

'So, what do you do, Levi?' Apart from watching me. Not that she was interested.

'I have a business in Sydney.'

She'd bet it wasn't a physical job because his hands looked too smooth and clean. She wasn't going to comment, even mentally, on his obvious fitness.

He raised his eyebrows. 'You have a very expressive face. By the curl of your lip I'm surprised you think I do anything.'

'I'm sure you're busy.' If he didn't want to tell her then that was fine. The less she knew about him the better. She turned her shoulder further away from him.

'My sister tells me you don't like helicopters much.'

Politeness meant she had to turn back. Hopefully he'd see her reluctance and leave her alone. 'Nothing personal to helicopters. I don't like to fly in anything.'

He shifted his shoulders so she was lined up with him again. 'Shame then. A pilot's license would be useful with the distances you have out here.'

Like Kate and her plane. She'd never feel comfortable to do that. 'My friend flies. I'll do without. My peace of mind.'

He acknowledged her aversion with a flick of his hand. 'It's a different world. Immediate, stunning, and even I admit this country is spectacular from the air.'

'Even you?' She felt her hackles rise and she sipped her drink before she said more. Needed to damp down her desire to demand he appreciate her home. 'The Kimberley Mountains are spectacular from the ground as well.'

He put his glass down. 'I've offended you again.'

'The bush is not for everyone.' She shrugged, added, 'Thankfully.' Not quietly enough.

'And you're happy about that?'

Could she offend him? Seemed not. 'There are advantages.'

A waiter appeared. It was time for dinner. Finally.

Levi gestured her towards the other end of the candlelit veranda, where a section of glass ceiling showcased the sky. In the dark it would be amazing with the stars. The table glowed with white linen, silver cutlery, and flowers. 'Gorgeous.'

'Very civilized,' Levi agreed, as if he were still surprised by it. Did he think they couldn't put on a good show up here in the bush?

She took her seat and they were joined by the resort manager, Steve, a handsome young man, more Odette's early twenties than Levi's mid-thirties.

Steve said and did all the right things and appeared anxious to ensure that Odette was safely seated or served as if she were an invalid. Baby phobia, Sophie guessed, but he left Sophie with a feeling of awkwardness she couldn't warm to.

The rapport between Levi and Odette showed genuine affection. Reluctantly Sophie admitted she liked that – family was important, so he had some redeeming features which she didn't really want to see. In fact, Levi proved himself a wonderful host. Then again, her ex, Brad, had been a great host too.

Odette remained animated and "William" held his own end of the conversation up for a change. So strange and unexpected for her brother.

Sophie had to rein herself in when she would normally have answered for Smiley until finally she subsided in awe at his previously hidden ability to socialize.

So, she sat back. The red wine helped. He could have come on his own after all. Great. Would have been nice to know that earlier.

Until the talk turned to helicopters.

'We should fly out to the Bungles.'

This she couldn't keep silent on. 'Not for me, thanks.'

Odette's disappointment seemed genuine. 'Just for a picnic. Once you try it, you'll love it.'

Smiley said, 'Sophie believes helicopters fall out of the sky.'

Levi sat back in his chair and smiled at her. 'No, they don't.'

Loosened up by the delightful Margaret River Shiraz, Sophie pointed her finger at him. 'So, tell me what happens when the engine stops in a helicopter.'

Her comment came in a lull and stilled all conversation. Levi tilted his head at her. 'They glide. Autorotation. Instead of the air being pulled in from the top by the engine, the rotors turn the other way and pull the air in from underneath as you descend. Gives the aircraft a forward and downward control. Forward like a winged airplane, just not as far.'

She didn't believe him. 'How far?'

'Enough to get passengers on the ground without falling.' He held her gaze, daring her to disbelieve him.

Sounded too simple. 'Then you can take off again?'

He rubbed his chin. 'Depends why it stopped. And maybe not always without hurting the chopper in the landing.' He seemed sure of his facts.

Sophie digested that.

'We've two helicopters at Xanadu,' Steve said, 'and never had a problem.' He smiled kindly at her and she felt patted like a small dog. Sophie wondered why the urge to wipe the smile off his face twitched her fingers. Maybe the poor guy had trained himself to be deprecating around his VIP guests but Sophie found his attentions irritating.

She glanced at Levi but she couldn't read anything in his face. Probably used to people fawning over him.

The conversation moved on and Sophie subsided to observe. Levi made no attempt to direct the conversation, he just did. She had to admit he was well educated and amusing and seemed to know the right thing to bring out the passion in Smiley for the land.

Sophie was surprised by her brother's friendly responses to their host and fought against her own mixed feelings as conversation swirled around her. It was fun and fascinating and she could feel the pull of Levi's charisma.

Sophie dragged her eyes away from Levi again and stared at her hands. She wanted to go home, or at least get out of this room away from him. But it wasn't polite to eat and run.

With the meal cleared away, Sophie drifted towards the end of the veranda where the steps led down to the path around the side of the homestead. The stars were out already and the further she moved away from the veranda the brighter the sky lights formed into the constellations and patterns she'd grown up with.

The Southern Cross, the Pot, the Milky Way. A wooden bench under a huge boab looked the perfect place to hide. She sank gratefully down on warm wood in the dimness, and the soft breeze rattled the boab leaves over her head as if to soothe her.

Until Levi strode out onto the veranda with his satellite phone and shattered the magic of the night along with the calm she'd achieved.

Brad had been like that. Needing to take every call. Oblivious to others when he was on the phone. Or like Brad, calling to check his woman was waiting patiently at home, while he dallied somewhere else.

She'd like to see Levi bogged in a bulldust hole with no handy phone. See how resourceful he'd be with nobody but himself to rely on.

No. She didn't want that. Heat could dehydrate and she'd have to put in a drip.

Then he saw her, ended the conversation and snapped his phone shut. She leant back into the shadows in a futile retreat as if he would forget she was there, slightly guilty about her mean thoughts for a man she barely knew, but still bitter by personal experience from the callousness of the man who had promised to love her and only her.

He paused at the bottom of the steps as if he could see Sophie didn't want company and was reluctant to force his own on her.

'Coffee is ready if you'd like some.' He glanced at the grass. 'Unless you'd prefer it out here?'

Guilt wormed. Bad guest. Not his fault.

She stood up and walked towards him with a swish of her blue dress. 'Thank you. Inside will be fine.'

Chapter 3

Levi stopped as he entered the room for breakfast on the veranda next morning. It seemed he'd interrupted an amusing show.

His sister, with much eye-batting and smiles, was trying to convince cowboy William to stay another day.

She was "desperate" that they should fly to the Bungle Bungles, a prehistoric massif of striped domes at the edge of the Tanami Desert, with a picnic basket, an idea which left a horrified expression on Sophie's face. Intriguing situation.

'We can picnic. I'm not pressuring Sophie. She can come or stay here with Levi and enjoy the resort. Pools, rainforest, lunch on the terrace is nice too.'

He could see a ride in the helicopter was the last thing Sophie wanted to do... No, make that second last. If he read her expression right when she glanced at him, the last thing she wanted was to stay behind at Xanadu, alone, with him.

Levi could read her like a road sign. Or a crocodile warning. That was amusing too. Sort of. Though he'd never had someone blatantly avoid his company before.

'I'll go,' Sophie said, but her false smile said she didn't want to.

He sat down next to her, maybe too deliberately close because he was a little miffed she so badly wanted to avoid him. His thigh didn't touch hers when he turned but he could almost feel her thrum with awareness. The fresh herby stuff she'd washed her hair with teased his nose and he wanted to close his eyes, lean in and inhale.

That would go over well as a space invasion.

He didn't lean. 'Good morning, Sophie.'

Her skin glowed golden in the morning light like the honey on the crumpet she nibbled with small white teeth. Which reminded him he'd spent more than a few hours in bed last night trying to banish her tenacious ghost. He must be having a crisis.

'Morning.' Her answer was accompanied by a darting look that came and went as she shrank her shoulders to avoid contact.

He had to bite back a smile. Becoming a habit those smiles. Very strange. 'Did you sleep well?'

'Fine, thanks.' Another flick of her eyes and he relented and shifted his chair a few inches away to give her some space.

Her delightful shoulders actually sank with relief and he wondered why he was playing with her. He wasn't normally pushy. 'Sorry,' he murmured, not intending to apologize but suddenly needing to.

Reluctantly she asked, 'Did you sleep well?' It seemed she could talk now he'd moved.

That smile tickled his mouth. 'No, not really. The symphony of the night seemed especially loud.'

She raised those stern brows of hers. 'Kept awake by nature? Poor you. Well it is a wilderness park.' She tossed her head. 'Sure beats the heck out of traffic noise.'

Maybe she didn't need sympathy. She could stand up for herself. After that they ate their meal in silence. Odette continued to flirt with Smiley.

Levi rubbed his chin as all stood to leave, because funnily enough her lack of enthusiasm for the flight made his skin itch.

'Odette?' he said, and his sister turned back. 'Look after Sophie. Remember she's not comfortable, so no stunts.'

Odette raised her eyebrows at him and saluted. 'Yes, sir.'

Sophie sent him a semi-grateful look over her shoulder as she dragged her feet to follow the other two to the helipad.

Levi frowned to himself as he went the other way. He needed to concentrate on the paperwork he had to get through before they returned to Sydney, but the ridiculously blue Kimberley sky outside the window invited sacrifice. Odette was too pregnant to be pilot. And Sophie looked unhappy.

Unhappy was too mild a word. Sophie didn't know how she'd agreed to this.

Now Steve, the resort manager, had shooed Odette away from pre-flight checks. 'I can't let a pregnant lady do that,' he said with that tilted smile that prickled right up Sophie's nose. There was something about him that tickled her memory but she couldn't connect the impression.

She'd never had much to do with the people from Xanadu, and apparently, he'd been here for a few years and had been very close to the late owner. She wished he'd mind his own business though.

To make matters worse, just before take-off, Levi appeared and decreed he'd pilot instead of Odette. Suddenly Sophie could have stayed behind. Talk about bad luck.

Everyone was looking out for Odette.

Which was a good thing but Sophie wondered if it was too late to look out for herself?

New seating arrangements meant she'd be up front next to Levi. This kept getting better and better. Not.

They all got out and reshuffled into their new seats.

The front of the helicopter was as bad as she'd imagined. She shrank back into the stiff leather seat, semi-frozen, not quite believing she'd agreed to this when Levi reached in from the outside to click her belt into place.

His hands pulled the belt firmly across her belly and snapped it shut. Talk about space invasion. This whole expedition was crazy and way out of her comfort zone. How the heck had she found herself next to him in a doorless chopper with only the seatbelt between her and certain death?

And on that note, surely there should have been more robust seatbelts or harnesses or something? One belt didn't seem enough.

Odette and Smiley chatted happily, ensconced in the rear out of sight and out of earshot. Once they got going, she thought bitterly, they'd be safe in their own little world. Exactly what Odette wanted.

Levi climbed in and she squashed herself back against the edge. He pointed to the bulky headphones hooked on the central support in front of her, and indicated she put them on.

'Can you hear me?' His metallic voice made her jump, and she looked across at him and glared. He nodded and she nodded facetiously back. He frowned then went on. 'It's automatically switched to receive, so for you to be heard by everyone else just press this button to speak.'

He withdrew his attention from her and glanced in the back. 'You guys all buckled up?'

Odette's voice crackled. 'Roger.'

Levi glanced around the deserted helipad and began the pre-flight sequence. 'All clear,' he said to no-one in particular and started the rotors.

The next few minutes Sophie missed as her eyes were tightly shut. The distant noise through the headphones grew noisier and she felt the shudder from the flimsy craft right through the backs of her knees, then the first sideways swish of movement through the air and then back the other way.

She opened one eye. It was too hard not to look. They swayed a little from side to side as they edged higher and she could see the downdraught from the rotors beating the bushes below.

Then she could see the river at the bottom of the gorge, the roof of the homestead, the tops of the trees, and it was all a little intriguing though she still pushed herself deep into her perch. She tried to relax her shoulders but the fear she'd fall out kept her rigid in the seat.

They climbed higher, and despite the lack of doors she was protected from the wind by the bubble of the front windshield, and actually it didn't feel too bad.

She opened the other eye. There was a Perspex floor in front of her feet. What sort of sick person designed a helicopter with a see-through floor? If she'd had eyes in the bottom of her soles she'd be able to look through the Perspex to the ground.

Basically she was standing on a thin edge above certain death. Her eyes closed at the vertigo of that thought, then opened again to risk a glance towards Levi as he concentrated on the dials at the front of the cockpit.

What was he looking at? Was everything okay?

She studied the instrument panel herself for something familiar. Maybe she'd even find a reassuring needle. Shame the guy wasn't more into smiling but at least he was taking the danger of the situation seriously.

Knots. They were doing eighty knots, and that was faster than mph, so fairly fast.

Fuel. There was seventy gallons of fuel. Tank was full, anyway. Guess that meant if they crashed she'd die in a ball of flame.

She looked away. Maybe don't read the dials. They'd climbed higher while she'd been contemplating the manner of their death, and she could look down on the escarpment now.

This was pretty amazing. And when she looked back, carefully, towards the homestead and the serpentine river, it made her appreciate how remote the properties were out here.

She'd flown on jets from Perth to Kununurra but they'd been much higher and she'd never really noticed individual stations, though mostly because she'd chosen the aisle seat and not the window.

'We'll fly up and over the waterfall on the property.' Levi's voice crackled through the headphones. 'Odette likes that and then over to Lake Argyle. We'll pass over a couple of stations Smiley asked to see, then in over the Bungles and back out over the Kimberley diamond mine and home.'

He was telling her this because...?

Her stomach sank. She pushed the button to speak. 'Sounds like a long flight. Do we land anywhere?'

His teeth flashed. He couldn't possibly be concentrating enough on his job if he could smile about it, she thought sourly. 'Anywhere you want,' he said.

She resisted saying, 'Here,' but not by much, and just nodded and turned away to glance at her watch. They'd be home in a few hours. She hoped.

Actually the next hour passed fairly quickly. The waterfall looked surreal from above with sparkling drops at the side of the main body of water shimmering on the breeze to the gorge below.

Lake Argyle loomed indigo blue and stretching forever, apparently seven times the size of Sydney Harbour, so that must be why it seemed to take seven times longer than she expected to cross.

When they flew over the isolation of the two cattle stations, Smiley asked Levi to circle again, so he could point out how they corralled their cattle using the land formations to form a natural bottleneck and arena. These were the stations Smiley had his eye on.

Sophie tried to concentrate on the implications of a station with no contact to the outside world during the wet season for at least four months, but all she could feel was the g-force of gravity pulling her towards the doorway. Her whole body seemed to be straining against the seat belt as they circled and she had this horrible feeling that maybe Levi hadn't fastened her buckle properly and she'd just pop out of it into spiraling space.

Now that was a dilemma. She hadn't checked the belt herself but if she touched it now she might press the eject button.

Come on. Their aircraft was circling thousands of feet above the hard earth and Smiley was going on about the logistical difficulties of cattle to market. It was no good.

'Can we land soon?' Sophie's voice cut across Smiley's, squeaky with distress, and she felt Levi's glance at her.

Immediately the helicopter levelled out. 'Bungles in fifteen minutes, you right with that?' Levi's voice was still tinny, but the strange thing was the lack of humor, just genuine understanding and concern in his voice and the reassurance she gained from that. His hand came across and rested on her upper arm as if to transfer calmness. From a man she didn't trust it shouldn't have helped that much. But it did. Like a lifeline.

Funny how she'd never felt that mixture of empathy and support from Brad's touch and she'd been engaged to him.

Inexplicably steadied, she nodded, and allowed herself to sag more into the seat and close her eyes. Think calm thoughts. Take deep breaths. Everything will be fine.

That was when the engine spluttered, coughed, and died. Her eyes flew open. The world seemed to stop.

Suddenly there was no background noise except the wind and the rotors turning without an engine. She watched in horror as Levi kept his hands glued to the controls correcting the cabin's inclination to yaw.

Levi's voice travelled down the tunnel of her frozen mind. 'Have to land fast.' His voice was much louder without the sound of the engine, then she couldn't hear him at all because he'd switched the radio from the cabin to transmit the distress call. But she could watch his lips move, grimly, as he enunciated their position.

Unwilling to stare frozenly out of the Perspex beneath her feet she kept her eyes on Levi.

Glide. Helicopters can glide like planes but not as far. She remembered him saying that. She believed him. But he did lie. Had he lied then, too? Surely not about this.

They weren't falling like a stone at the moment, still going forward, but the altimeter was unwinding like a top, much, much faster than it had wound up.

Then she remembered that Odette and Smiley were in the back but she couldn't turn her neck to look. They'd all die. Odette's baby, too.

No. They had to survive. That thought steadied her. She was the midwife. The only medical person. They'd need her. Odette's baby needed her. She'd better survive intact.

She stared at Levi who looked as if his face were hewn from the same stone as the escarpment they hurtled towards as he wrestled with the controls. No panic, just fierce, implacable determination to win. Thank God he'd decided to be the pilot. Even now he inspired confidence.

Then there was no time for thoughts. Just the sickening rush of the ground towards them and she tucked her chin onto her chest and hugged her knees so she must have listened to all those hostesses on flights she'd tried to block out. Thank you, hostesses.

They were coming in too fast.

The impact flung her head back as the helicopter slammed into the ground. Someone screamed and she wasn't sure if it was Odette or herself, then they clipped a boulder and the cabin flipped up and tipped sideways and landed once more with a larger crash and finally, with agonizing slowness tipped back to crash back on its base with a rattle of rocks and debris. They'd stopped. Intact.

That first few seconds of cessation of movement was more frightening than the seconds before where at least she'd known she was alive.

She straightened her aching neck to look at Levi.

He didn't move, his long lashes were resting on ashen cheeks, and for a horrific moment she thought he was dead. Then she saw the rise and fall of his chest and the release made the nausea rise in her throat.

She reached across for his hand that lay limply pointed at her and felt for his pulse. It was fast but steady and she heaved a sigh of relief.

A soft moan from behind her. Gingerly, she turned her head. 'Odette? Smiley? You both alright?'

'I think William's unconscious. What about Levi?'

'His pulse is strong but he's out too. We hit some scrub on their side of the aircraft so I think they bore the brunt of it.' She didn't know whether to ask or not. 'Your baby? Everything alright there?'

'I think so.' Odette's voice cracked. 'We need to get out. Get them out. The fuel!'

Sophie's fingers grappled with her belt clasp. The locking mechanism wouldn't open and those ball-of-flame visions returned to add desperation to her frustration. She rattled the catch.

Levi's hand came across and pushed the release and suddenly she was free. 'It's okay. I'll do it.'

Why was he whispering? At least he was conscious. Thank God. 'You were knocked out.'

'Hmm,' he said, his voice still weak, and rubbed the back of his head. Then he blinked and sat up straighter. 'You okay? Out!' He turned his attention to the back seat but Odette was already on the ground and attempting to rouse Smiley.

Sophie scrambled up from her seat and climbed over the scattered wreckage at the front of the craft to help Odette. Smiley groaned but didn't open his eyes and Sophie lifted his lids to peer into his eyes. His pupils contracted with the light and she heaved a sigh of relief. No time for sympathy. 'Wake up, Smiley. Move!'

Smiley's eyelids fluttered and he groaned. 'What happened?'

Levi was out and beside them now, too. He swayed ever so slightly and Sophie watched him with narrowed eyes. 'Later, sport,' Levi said. 'Let's get you out of here, though I think if the tank was going to explode it would have done before now.' He shooed both women with his hand. 'Get away, over by those trees you two. Now.'

Odette turned and hobbled away but Sophie stood her ground. 'Maybe he shouldn't be moved.'

'No choice.' Levi frowned at Smiley. 'Can you move your fingers and toes?'

'My leg hurts.'

'No tingling?'

Smiley shook his head, then grimaced, and tried to pull himself free, but recoiled his arm back to his chest with a loud groan.

The hiss of liquid hitting hot metal made them all jump. Levi frowned. 'I'll do the work, just brace your arm.' And he heaved Smiley sideways and onto the ground in one huge movement and then dragged him away from the aircraft with Sophie almost glued to his back. The intermittent hiss from behind hastened their steps.

Sophie looked back over her shoulder. 'I'm glad it only just started doing that.'

Levi propped Smiley against a tree. 'I could have lived without it. We'll give it some time to cool down and then see what's happening with the radio as long as everyone is stable.'

He turned to his sister who hovered over Smiley. 'What about you, Odette? Your baby?'

'I'm not hurt. He's moving normally. Is William alright?'

'Fine. I'm more worried about you.' He looked at Sophie who nodded and drew his sister to a fallen tree to sit.

'You need to sit for a while, Odette. We've fallen out of the sky.' She shook her head. Holy Moley. 'We're alive but it's crazily worse than a car accident and babies don't like being in those. You sure you're not contracting?'

Odette stroked her belly. 'It doesn't hurt.'

'Okay. But sit while I check Smiley.'

'His name is William,' Odette said. 'Smiley sounds like a dummy and he's not that.'

Sophie blinked. Good grief. That's all she needed. 'William,' she said but rolled her eyes as she turned away.

Chapter 4

L evi glowered at the wreckage of the aircraft and shook his head as they all gathered their breath. 'An engine should never do that.' His jaw clamped tight and she could see the implacable leader who highly resented mechanical failure.

Well, yes. She wasn't too impressed about it herself but even she knew the unexpected was possible.

Nobody else said anything and Sophie asked the question. 'What happened?'

Levi ignored her and turned to his sister. 'You saw nothing out of order in the pre-flight check, Odette?'

His sister grimaced. 'I only started it, Steve finished it.'

'Did he?' Levi's face stilled. 'It's not your fault.' He spoke very quietly and Sophie frowned as she tried to gather the thread of undertones and make sense of it, but for some reason the hairs on her arms prickled and stood and she lifted her arms across her chest to rub them.

Levi was muttering. 'I can't believe I didn't do my own pre-flight as well as yours. You should never do anything last minute when flying. No excuses. First rule of flight.'

'What now?' Odette asked.

He glanced at the sky. 'We're baking in the sun. We need more shade and definitely water. I'll go up the gorge to see if there's a creek or a pool.'

Levi to the rescue? She didn't think so. 'Let me. As soon as I've checked on Sm—' she glanced at Odette and corrected herself '—William.'

Levi looked pale; a purple bruise had begun on his temple and she could see him blaming himself when he'd saved them all. Sophie went on. 'You've been knocked out. You should move to the shade and I'll find the water.'

She'd avoided his eyes while she spoke and flicked a glance back to see how he took her suggestion. Not well, judging by the scowl he directed at her.

He straightened, until he loomed over her, but the effect was spoiled when he swayed slightly. 'Who died and elected you captain? I can make my own decisions, thanks.'

Sophie shrugged that off. He didn't intimidate her. Grumpy sod. 'It's a small job. As I'm the only medical person and you look like death warmed up, I say you need to rest after your heroics earlier. You're still the captain, just a concussed one, so that's what you'll do.'

He blinked, didn't quite drop his mouth open but she knew she'd surprised him. He looked about to say something but didn't, shaking his head slightly instead.

Sophie glanced at Odette and lowered her voice. 'Someone needs to keep an eye on your sister and give me a yell if she complains of any pain, too, though I won't be long.' She looked at her brother. 'But William first.'

Levi hovered while she examined Smiley and it was hard to ignore him. She'd have liked to tell him to sit again but didn't want to push her luck. She doubted anyone had tried to tell him what to do since he was in school. It would do him good. Actually thinking of him as a scrubby schoolboy did a lot for her confidence.

She spoke to William. 'How's the head?' She ran her fingers lightly over the swelling under his right eye and then palpated the bulge over his ear. 'You've given it a good whack. Close your eyes for a couple of seconds and then open them.'

He did so and she watched his pupils constrict at the light. They looked equal as much as she could tell.

She checked his ears for discharge but there was none, and it made her think she should do the same for Levi. She looked at him.

'My ears are fine,' he said quickly, 'and I'm sure my pupils are too.'

Sophie shrugged. 'Your choice,' she said, not eager for another clash of wills, and looked back at William.

'You've dislocated the shoulder again?' A sister's tone.

William grimaced. 'I'd say.'

'We can fix that. We've done it before.' But she really didn't want to think about doing that. 'And the ankle?'

'Pretty sore.'

They all looked at it, swollen already, and she ran her hands over it but couldn't feel any blatant deviations of line. Poor Smiley. 'That's gotta hurt. We'll splint it, get you a walking stick and at least you'll be independent for short walks. You still wear your knife?'

He nodded and patted his hip with his good hand.

'Good,' she said, and looked at him with sympathy for the impending pain. 'You want to do the shoulder now before it swells more?'

'Quicker the better.' Tight-lipped but still brief.

Sophie looked at Levi. 'Can you help me with this?'

Levi appeared even more dubious. 'You sure you know what you're doing?'

Did he think she did this stuff for fun? 'I've done it for William twice before.' And hated it.

Levi opened his mouth and then closed it again. 'If he's got faith in you then I'm happy to help. Just tell me what you want me to do.' Deferring to her? Not what he'd said a minute ago but she didn't think it a good time to point that out.

He still looked uncomfortable and she wondered if he was feeling faint again. 'You sure you're okay, Levi?'

'I'm fine.' The terse man was back. He looked at William. 'What about his pain relief.'

She shook her head. 'The sooner I line the bones up again so they'll slide back in, the better. And he's been knocked out anyway. Not a good idea.'

Sophie took a deep breath and hoped everyone couldn't see how sick this made her. She knelt down beside William and cleared the dirt in front of him of rocks and sticks for him to lie down.

She'd need a piece of material to go around William's chest and under his injured armpit that Levi could pull on while she manipulated William's arm. It needed to be strong like clothing. Probably her blouse would be best. Though, it could be Levi's shirt. She thought about that and decided she didn't want to see his chest. She had a fair idea the picture might lodge in her brain.

'We'll use my shirt.' She turned around before anyone could say anything and slipped it off. Businesslike, as if she wasn't really sitting there in front of them all in her lacy bra, and she refused to think about whether she had little rolls of belly as she bent over.

This day just kept getting better and better.

She spread her shirt on the ground to roll the material up in a long sausage and slipped it around Smiley's body and under his armpit until the two ends met back on Levi's side.

'Down you go, William. Shuffle forward so you can stretch out on your back.' Smiley eased down with agonized slowness. She looked at Levi. 'Just kneel down facing him on the uninjured side and hold the ends firmly like handles.'

Levi knelt beside Smiley and concentrated on the task as he gathered the ends.

Why they crashed could wait. He should be doing this, not her, but it didn't seem the right moment to pull rank on her. It had been a lot of years since he'd done any generalist work like dislocations. He bet she'd be wild to learn that his "business" was medicine.

She was directing them like an annoying but perky little conductor in her bra and shorts and he liked her more than when she'd been sexily annoying in her blue dress. As she bent towards William her breasts fell his way. In a gesture of respect he faded out her cleavage, which was no mean feat, and watched her hands.

She surprised him with her calmness and methodical approach to something he could probably have done but not as confidently as she did. Qualifications meant zip against recent experience, he reassured himself.

Sophie nodded. 'Keep both ends together under his good armpit. When I take his other arm you keep the pressure on his chest so he can't follow me.'

Levi could hear his sister mumbling behind him as she agonized over Smiley's impending discomfort. He wished she'd be quiet.

Sophie must have heard her too. 'He'll be fine, Odette. I know we're all still shell-shocked from the crash but he'll be okay.' Sophie looked his way. 'As long as Levi doesn't tickle him 'cause it hurts to laugh.'

Levi blinked in surprise at her comment and compressed his lips to bite back the smile. Effective stress relief. She was a tough little cookie, though he'd begun to wonder if she really was as tough as she made out, because he could detect a tiny tremor in her hands every now and then. 'Nurses have a dreadful sense of humor, eh William?'

Smiley had his eyes shut. 'Hmm.'

But the tension had lessened a little and even Odette got the hint to relax.

He watched Sophie's face as she concentrated. Something made him want to reach out and touch her arm, just for support, like he had during the flight when he realized she'd started to panic, but he didn't want to interrupt her thoughts or her process.

It was almost as if she rehearsed the steps.

Sophie knelt down and after a brief finger stroke of sympathy she took her brother's elbow and gently bent it so that his fingers pointed to the sky they'd just fallen from. She didn't even want to think about sky-falling.

Bend arm at ninety-degree angle from his body, Sophie recited to herself.

'Keep the pressure on now,' she said quietly to Levi, and began to pull – still gently but firmly – on the bent elbow, away from William's body while keeping the forearm at a ninety-degree angle to his body.

Then she rotated the arm on the shoulder joint as if William was trying to throw a baseball.

Sweat beaded on William's forehead as she moved it slowly back and forward until the shoulder slid back into place with a click that made everyone wince.

'Okay.' Now Sophie felt like crying or heaving or running away but she couldn't do any of those things. 'We need a sling.'

She looked at William and he gave her a small wink. 'Thanks, Sis.'

'Don't do it again. You know I hate it.' She dropped a kiss on his forehead and Levi was there to help her stand. She hadn't even noticed he'd moved and secretly she was glad of his support because her legs wobbled.

Levi's hand kept hold of hers and he pulled her gently into his chest for a moment in a purely asexual embrace though his shirt against her nose meant she could only inhale air laced with Levi. His arms rested around her back, firmly but not cloying, and just for that moment she rested her head on him and closed her eyes to regroup.

Strangely, the hug wasn't an invasion of space as much as a recoup of resources and exactly what she needed.

She stepped back and his arms fell. 'Thanks. I hate doing that for him.' She astounded herself with the honesty and he looked just as surprised. Normally she wouldn't let anyone know when she felt overwhelmed.

Sophie felt proud of her self-sufficiency and she would have thought Levi was the last person she'd want to tell about any weakness on her part. Had to be part of the shock of the crash.

She watched his hands flick the dirt from her shirt and smooth it and then he held it out for her to slip her arms in. She felt strangely cosseted but weepy. Not something she was used to at all. She didn't like the feeling.

'Well done, Sophie,' he said quietly.

She couldn't meet his eyes in case he saw the glitter of tears in hers. She stared at her shirt in his hands. 'Umm. I need to tear a bit off the bottom to make a sling.'

He shook his head. 'Put it on. Mine's bigger. You don't want to get a sunburnt strip around your waist.'

She took it and turned away to collect herself.

A hug was okay but sympathy when she was emotional was such a pain. She sniffed unobtrusively. Men were so good at that. Twisting the knife when you were trying to gain control.

She heard the rip of his shirt as he made the sling, kept her eyes averted and took a couple of deep breaths, then turned back to face the group. To her surprise Levi had achieved a very creditable sling.

'Distinction in a First Aid course, eh?' she said in a poor attempt of a joke. She saw the look from Odette. Followed by Levi's shake of the head but Sophie was too tired to care about that.

'Something like that.' He looked at William. 'So how's the shoulder now?'

'Good as new.' They all knew he lied.

Levi gave him a crooked smile. 'I'll bet.' He glanced at Sophie. 'I can do splints and bandages but we'll do that after you check we have a water supply.'

'Yes, Captain,' she couldn't resist saying. 'Next time we come into land here, I'll try to have a look as we approach.'

'Good idea.' He stood up. 'There's a couple of water bottles in the chopper. I'll get them and check the radio if everything's cooled down enough.' He rubbed his chin. 'But I'll come with you. After I discuss something with Odette.'

Sophie sighed. He was determined then. His funeral. She had to stop saying that. It was obviously a bad omen.

Levi hadn't been keen for her to hang around the wreck so she wandered slowly towards the gully, pleased to have a moment before he joined her. The chance to walk away from the crash site was welcome and she dawdled along the gorge watching the ground for signs of animals. She didn't hear him come up beside her and she jumped when he spoke.

'You think we'll find water?'

She glanced at him. 'Pretty confident.'

'Fine,' he said, but raised his brow skeptically.

She frowned. 'The wet season's not long finished, and rock pools and depressions in the gorge floor should still hold water.'

She should know. She'd walked so many gorges in her lifetime apparently preparing for just such an occasion. Hopefully, the water wouldn't be too old, either, but there'd be enough to keep them until help arrived. Which shouldn't be long if the distress call went through.

As they walked, long grey-green grasses poked out at them, and as they brushed past Sophie inhaled the warm air and everything felt brighter and cleaner... and even more precious for nearly being snatched away.

'I can't believe how close we came to dying back there.' Yet as she walked away from the site with this man, somehow, he lessened the horror. That they'd all managed to escape fairly unscathed so far was a miracle, and she knew their lives had depended on Levi's determination they would survive.

Levi didn't say anything. The taciturn man from the Pentacost church was back. She'd forgotten him. But, they were alive. He needed to smell the roses.

'We're standing in one of the most fascinating geological landmarks in the world. It reminds you these towers are millions of years in creation, doesn't it?'

He turned to give her a flat stare. 'No, Pollyanna. It reminds me we've had to force land in the middle of nowhere with very little to keep us alive.'

She knew about survival out here. As did Smiley. She frowned at him. 'Lighten up. The Aboriginal people survived.' Sophie spread her arms. 'You'll see that in the overhangs and caves. Stories to read on the rock. They've been a part of this land for thousands of years. We'll manage a day or two.'

He lifted his eyes to the sky as if praying. 'Spare me from eternal optimism.'

She checked her directions. Muttered, 'And me from a grump.'

She was only a hundred meters from the plane when she found the break in the range she was looking for. They looked back before they turned into a narrow gorge off the main escarpment, but Odette and Smiley were still sitting on the boulders where they'd left them.

It was cool in the gully, the sun not yet directly overhead to shine onto the narrow strip of valley floor. 'It would be worthwhile moving the others here to get out of the sun,' she commented. 'We should probably move here soon if we have to wait long for rescue.'

'I would have suggested that. You beat me to it.'

She slanted an amused glance at him. 'I'm annoying you then?'

'Not at all.'

Liar, she thought, but she didn't say it.

Tufts of sharp Spinifex scratched at her ankles as she scrambled over boulders that had tumbled down from the walls and Levi followed her. Within minutes she'd come upon the first pool and she raised her brows at him. This was her backyard and she'd proved it. See?

'Okay, good.' he said. 'Water. Looks a bit green though.'

'It's just starting to algae, but the middle of the pool will be clear and no doubt cold.'

He didn't look convinced.

'It's a good time of the year if you have to crash,' she teased him. 'Those tiny fish don't know their pond will disappear over the next few months.'

'I guess fish prove the water's clean enough to drink.'

'Yep. The traditional owners use bunches of sharp Spinifex to brush the pools and capture the tiny fish in the barbs. Then they burn it and eat the fish. We might try that later.'

She crouched at the edge to fill her bottle, peripherally aware of the snake trail to her left. The smooth indent in the fine gravel was a timely reminder to watch for basking reptiles. She had a feeling that her city-slicker companion wasn't ready to know that yet.

Chapter 5

Levi couldn't believe this woman. She talked as if they were film-ing for a nature show, not about their survival in one of the most remote places in the world.

She sat back and glanced around as she screwed the lid back on the water bottle, then washed her hands before bathing her face and lower arms. His eyes were drawn to the way she slid the water over the inside of her wrists and then lifted her fingers to allow the trickles to run down her neck and beneath the collar of her blouse.

Hastily he leaned forward and rinsed his own hands. It was cold alright, just what he needed after the heat on the valley floor. Not to mention the other heat.

'Right. We have water and a few tiny fish to eat. Our own bush-tucker chef. It could be worse.'

'Not sure how.'

'We're alive.'

He nodded soberly. True. All of them and that was a miracle. No thanks to the person who'd tampered with the aircraft, and the concept still had the power to make him livid enough to want to crush a rock with his bare hands.

She must have noticed the intensity of his frown because she flicked a tiny drop of water at him. 'Don't suppose you fancy a witchetty grub. They're like crunchy caterpillars They taste like eggs. I can see a witchetty tree and I could dig the roots up for you.'

He had to smile. Retribution could wait. 'Pass.'

When they returned to the crash site the full extent of their miracle of survival made itself scarily plain. She stood for a moment and shook her head and he silently agreed.

Pieces of the helicopter were strewn like rubbish from a dog-chewed refuse bag. The cabin itself looked more like a drink can that had been beaten by a stick than a mode of travel.

The others had moved a few feet back against the canyon wall out of the sun, and sat on boulders that had fallen from the cliffs. 'You'd have to be unlucky, but I'm not sure I'd feel real comfortable waiting for another boulder to fall where they're sitting.'

Levi nodded. 'We'll move to the gorge as soon as I empty the aircraft.'

They separated, he to the aircraft and she to Odette.

Levi spread the first aid kit and the toolbox out on the ground to see what was available and he looked up as Sophie laughed out loud at something Odette had said.

At least someone could laugh about the situation they were in. His eyes were drawn when she stood up and approached his work area. Her white shirt had smudges of dust and her disarranged hair looked similar to the spinifex tufting the bottom of the canyon.

Actually, she looked pretty fantastic, considering she'd had her worst nightmare confirmed by a crash landing.

He'd been mulling over her behavior since the crash while he worked and he'd come to the conclusion he'd never met a woman like her.

Her composure when she'd reduced her brother's shoulder still impressed him. A better job than he would have done. It was far too long since he'd done any emergency work apart from eyes and he was glad he hadn't had to practice on Smiley.

His lack of disclosure about his medical background had become an elephant in their outdoor room he could've done without, but it didn't seem the right moment to correct the false impression he'd given. Hopefully, when he did, she'd just laugh it off. Unlikely though, if that first conversation they'd had at Xanadu was anything to go by. The longer he left it the bigger the elephant grew, but he really didn't have the capacity to take on a discussion of his work.

Still, she looked pretty pleased with herself and it was a bonus to find something to smile about after what he'd just discovered. 'Odette feels better?' Levi asked.

'Yep. And Smiley's fine.'

'That's great.' He paused. 'Do you want the good news or the bad news?'

Her smile died and he regretted that, but he wasn't joking. 'Can I have bad and then good to cheer me up?' she asked reluctantly.

'The bad news is the radio's dead.'

'That's really bad.' Her face fell further. 'And the good news?'

'The good news is the aircraft wouldn't have gone up in flames, because the fuel tank was on empty.'

He watched her think about that until finally she asked, 'Then what was the hissing?'

She had a logical mind. He liked that. Very much. 'The oil dripping on the hot engine.'

A tiny line crinkled between her brows. 'But how could the fuel be on empty? I saw it full on the gauge.'

He had an idea but it wasn't a very nice one. 'Must have sprung a leak.'

The crinkle deepened, and actually she looked cute, but it sure wasn't the time to notice that. 'Do fuel tanks do that?'

Never in his lifetime. He sighed. 'Not usually.'

He watched her shake her head – a lot of that head shaking had been going on around here – and he wished he didn't have to explain the rest. He gave her a minute to mull it over and looked at the minimal supplies they had to survive on. Not a lot there – the picnic basket which should be much more substantial considering where it came from; just some basic sandwiches, some chocolate bars, and thankfully, a dozen bottles of water - which was what he'd had a quick word to Odette about before he'd left with Sophie.

'You said the radio's dead. Why is that?'

He appreciated how calmly she'd taken his first news. Hysterics would have really done his head in. 'I'd like to know that too.'

He saw the beginnings of comprehension as her eyes widened. 'What are you saying? I saw you talk to someone as we were landing. I saw your lips move.'

He remembered that moment. It hadn't been pleasant. 'I wish I could offer more but I can't. I didn't get a response. I gave the position in case they could hear me even though I couldn't hear them. I don't know if it worked.'

She made a silent O with her mouth, her face like a book. Readable. No subterfuge. No doubt she'd scorn such a thing. She was so different from any woman he'd met and with such a well of strength that was scary.

'It was a good idea, anyway,' she said earnestly, as if sorry he felt bad. Now she made him smile. That was twice now. Then she said, 'But you've got one of those little GPS tracker things, don't you?'

'ELT. Emergency locator transmitter.' She didn't like what she saw on his face and he watched her transfer her attention to Odette for a more palatable answer.

Odette looked up. 'It seems someone took it out and didn't replace it,' Odette said baldly.

'Someone? Took it out?' Sophie actually squeaked and suddenly he wanted to put his arm around her but she backed away as if she knew what he was thinking. How could she know that?

She looked at her brother but all William did was shrug his good shoulder and not comment. Levi admired him for it. There wasn't much to say as the choices were limited.

Someone had tried to kill them and nearly succeeded.

None of the three of them mentioned the fact the chopper had been tampered with, but it simmered there between them, except that Sophie, still focused on the radio not working, didn't get it. No bonus in her knowing.

Sophie sank down on one of the boulders she hadn't wanted to sit on and, as an afterthought, handed a water bottle to each of them. She closed her eyes, sighed, and visibly relaxed her shoulders. Finally, she mumbled, 'Glad I'm not the captain.' Opened her eyes and looked straight at him. 'What's the plan... Captain?'

'Now she defers,' he said, but he was inordinately glad of her support. He wasn't quite sure when she'd stopped being annoying.

'William says he knows this area from mustering and there's an Aboriginal community a day's walk away if we head north. I'm thinking William and Odette should stay here, and you and I walk out and get help.'

She chewed her lip and glanced around the desolate landscape. 'It's breaking the first rule. Leaving the site. We're not that far from the desert and the sun's a furnace in the sky until five.' She looked at the supplies. 'But there's not a lot to eat out here once we get through the picnic basket.'

'My thoughts exactly.'

She narrowed her eyes. 'If we give them today to send a search party, staying put is a good thing.' She looked at his sister, and Levi had to keep from shaking his head in disbelief. She seemed so calm about the whole bloody thing. 'How do you feel about that, Odette?' she asked. As if it a mundane cancellation of an appointment.

He watched his sister struggle to match her composure and he wished, fruitlessly, he'd been firmer when she'd been so determined to leave Sydney with him.

Odette brushed the hair off her forehead. 'William can't walk far and I'm not much better. As long as we have water and a bit of food we'll be fine for a day, I guess.'

Sophie nodded and he thanked God again he'd been stranded with sensible people. He wondered if all of the people who lived out here in the back of beyond were like Sophie and William. Apart from the fact that maybe someone was trying to kill his sister and him – although that was unproven – the place was growing on him.

'I suggest we leave tomorrow morning, early. Do you agree?' Sophie said.

He almost smiled again. She couldn't help being bossy, though he suspected she'd push herself harder than anyone else. 'Sounds like a plan.'

She nodded and stood up. 'What would you like me to do?'

Yep. He'd been right. 'We'll collect wood first for a signal fire, then some for the camp tonight.'

'Sure.' Sophie stopped beside Odette again. 'No pains?' He could almost see the priorities ticking off in her mind.

Odette shook her head but her hand slid protectively over her stomach as if to ward off the idea. William reached over with his good arm and caught her fingers and held them. Odette squeezed back.

'I'd hate to be the one who's pregnant,' Smiley said.

Levi looked at Sophie. He'd been avoiding that horror. Unfortunately, he knew the danger to his sister lay in the sudden deceleration of their landing. Forces that could tear an inelastic placenta off an elastic uterus. He'd seen that in the brief time he'd had in obstetrics, but there was nothing they could do at this moment except watch her.

Sophie crouched down, obviously thinking the same thing because she said, 'So, how long since we crashed?'

'I thought it was a forced landing.' Levi pretended to be offended.

'My bad. How long since we auto-rotated?' she said over her shoulder as she faced Odette. 'How long is it since your incredible brother managed to avert disaster and get us to the ground safely, Odette?'

There was humor in the words but none in her voice. She meant every word and he was surprised how they unexpectedly warmed the place that had iced over with the knowledge of foul play. He'd never thought of himself as needing praise and he stamped the feeling out.

Odette looked at her watch. 'It feels like minutes but about an hour and a half.'

Sophie crouched and her hand hovered above Odette's uterus. 'May I?' She waited for permission, then rested her hand on the baby bulge. 'I'm thinking the first four hours are the most likely time you'd start contracting if there'd been any problems with the landing. It's fabulous you haven't gone into labor already. But tell me if you get regular pains.'

Odette shook her head as if by denying it, it wouldn't happen. 'Don't wish that on me.'

Sophie shook her head vehemently. 'I'm not. Believe me. Really not. The longer it holds off the less likely your baby has any ill effects from the events.'

Odette chewed her lip as she stroked her belly. 'It's not quite the serene home birth I'd envisaged.'

Sophie rolled her eyes. 'It's not the day any of us envisaged, except maybe me when we took off.' She smiled ruefully. 'And I apologize for that if I brought us all bad luck.'

Not the person to blame. 'If it was someone's fault,' Levi said dryly, 'It certainly wasn't yours.' He stood up. 'I used to be a pretty mean boy scout so reckon I could manage a fire in case a plane flies over.'

'Then I'll start collecting wood.' Sophie looked around. 'We'll need a campfire and a signal fire, right?'

Odette wiped her face. 'It's so hot. Hard to imagine we'll need heat.'

'It'll be cold tonight, once the sun goes down,' Smiley offered and squeezed Odette's hand.

Poor Smiley. He'd hate being unable to help. Sophie was glad he was there for Odette. She had the feeling if he hadn't been, Odette would have succumbed to hysterics by now and that would not have been fun.

To give the young mum her due, she was a city girl and where they'd crashed was as far as she'd get from a city.

Odette scuffed at the dry grass beneath her feet. 'What if we start a bushfire?'

'As long as it blows the other way it's all good,' Smiley said and, with his one good arm, spread the map Levi had given him from the wreck.

He didn't enlarge so Sophie finished the sentence. 'In the Kimberley bushfires are a way of life. We try to burn off the whole area every couple of years. Even as far out as here. The Aboriginal people have been burning off for thousands of years. For them it means the scrub stays sparse and they can see the animals they want to hunt.'

'Wow, I didn't know that,' Odette mused.

Sophie gestured with her hand. 'A lot of the trees and shrubs around here don't germinate until they've been through a fire. From our point of view, frequent fires germinate the land and prevent a massive fire that would be impossible to control.'

Odette gazed around at, what was to her, desolate landscape. 'It's so sparse and different from anywhere I've ever been,' Odette said, in much the same tone as if they'd landed on the moon.

She'd been the one keen to fly here for a picnic. But Sophie didn't say it. 'William and I love it.'

Sophie thought of Perth for the first time that day, actually the first time since she'd seen Levi. Now that did seem odd. But a happy loss. 'Perth's a pretty place. Has the ocean and sunset all in one,' she said trying to be fair, but Brad lived there and she'd gone off it. 'I wouldn't live anywhere else than here, though.'

She looked at Levi as she spoke and remembered his appreciation of her land was confined to flying over it.

He raised his brows. 'Don't look at me like that. Beautiful, sure, but you have great rivers and can't swim in them. Apparently it's the same in the ocean up here.'

Same old argument tourists always had. 'We have rock pools and gorges that are fine for swimming. You just have to know where is safe. We're fine here from crocs but watch for snakes as we walk.'

Levi glanced at his horrified sister and made a strangled sound. Had he just laughed at her?

'I hate snakes,' Odette shuddered, and she pulled closer to William.

'If you see one, just stop. Then back off real slow,' her brother drawled.

Sophie added, 'They panic too. They're just as likely to run the same way as you do.'

'It won't be really chasing me. Sure.' Odette shuddered.

Levi's gaze had stayed on her. Watching. She'd swear he was amused even though his mouth didn't move. He said, 'So, you're a snake lover too?'

'No, but it's their home. We're the intruders.' Sophie shook her head. 'Someone once told me that a snake has a really short memory, about forty seconds, which always makes me smile when I see one. I imagine them forgetting I'm there.'

After that, when they moved up next to the mouth of the gully, Odette's head swiveled like one of those toy nodding dogs people used to sit on the back window of their cars. She walked with Levi, her hand tightly gripped to his arm.

Smiley leaned heavily on his stick with Sophie on his other side. He said out of the corner of his mouth to Sophie, 'I feel so bloody useless.'

She whispered back. 'You're helping Odette which is great. She needs your calm. Will you manage when we go?'

Smiley looked around to ensure the others weren't in earshot. 'As long as she doesn't have the baby.'

Sophie whispered, 'It's just like a calf, Smiley, or a foal.'

He choked back a laugh. 'Great.' They grinned at each other. 'You'll run through a couple of things with me before you leave, though?' he asked.

She nodded. She had to believe Odette wouldn't go into labor in the day they'd be away. It was too frightening a thought. Not that there was anything they could change.

Smiley examined the spot she'd chosen, almost a cave, and nodded. 'At least up here I can get my own water.'

'It'll be tricky but you could.'

Levi came up to them with a long branch of dead wood he'd picked up on the way. 'We'll be out of the weather if one of the sudden tropical storms blows up.'

The able-bodied pitched in and there was a lip of overhang just past the entrance where they packed their supplies against the wall.

The afternoon passed as they watched for rescue, without reward, and prepared for the night.

Back out in the main canyon they'd erected a signal fire with green leaves on top for smoke as a way to flag down a search plane if one flew over them, but the sky remained clear of aircraft.

They wouldn't be missed at Xanadu until almost nightfall. They'd told Steve they'd be back by late afternoon so they were not technically even missing yet.

Levi began to cut the long grass that Sophie suggested they use for beds for the night, while she cleared the ground in front of the overhang so they could make a fire to keep everyone warm. With the wall behind them the heat would be caught and the flames would keep any animals away.

At four o'clock they sat back and Sophie could see the activity had raised Odette's spirits. 'I'd say we're a clever bunch. We could make it on one of those television survivor shows.'

'Except there's no camera man with a satellite phone.' Odette looked at the depleted picnic basket. 'Who wants to go to the shop for a treat?'

Sophie spread her arms. 'There's plenty to eat around here.'

Levi dropped the last of the sticks for the night fire. 'Spare me from Pollyanna with bush tucker,' Levi said. 'Not Witchetty grubs, I hope.'

Sophie refused to be downcast by the lack of enthusiasm. 'Must admit I've never been a fan of the old grub, though they say ten grubs a day is enough for survival.'

'Choice,' Levi said. 'That'd be Man Vs Wild.'

'Never heard of it. But I did find a Gubinge tree up one of the gullies. I'll show you where, before dark, in case you want some tomorrow, Odette.'

She held up the small greenish-yellow fruit which looked more like a pale pecan nut than a fruit. 'Known also as a Kakadu Plum, it's easy to eat.'

Smiley sat quietly amused during her explanations and declined to sample the fruit.

She frowned at him for not offering support but no doubt he still felt sick and sore. Not that he was complaining. He never did. Actually nobody complained so maybe she should revise her opinion about city people.

She directed her attention to Levi and Odette and bit bravely into the skin. The tanginess twisted on her tongue and she fought to keep her face straight as she chewed and swallowed. 'Food for indigenous people for thousands of years and apparently has a hundred times more vitamin C than an orange.'

She licked her lips and tried to define the taste. 'The juice crosses between a pear and an apple. There's a zing which I think is from the vitamin C but see what you think.' She tossed one each to Odette and Levi. 'Either way it's the perfect refreshment if we're right out of grocery shops.'

'Bush tucker.' Levi looked at her from under his brows as if to say are you having us on? When she nodded encouragingly he bit into the fruit, and then finished it off. 'Not addictive, but not bad.'

Sophie nodded. 'We'll take some with us when we walk out.'

'Something to look forward to.' He rubbed his hands together with fake enthusiasm.

So, he did have a sense of humor.

Chapter 6

Just before dawn the next morning, when the night birds were settling and the morning budgerigars shared their chatter, Levi and Sophie prepared to leave camp.

The gentle breeze lifted the bumps on Sophie's arms and the ground crackled cold and hard beneath her socks. She tucked her chin into her collar as she pulled on her boots. Smiley scowled as he'd handed over his prized possession. He held Levi's baseball cap as if it had teeth.

She glanced across to where Levi wore the broad Akubra and looked disturbingly like an R. M. Williams kinda man rather than the Levi city slicker she didn't trust. Much more dependable and much more hazardous to her peace of mind.

Then again, there wasn't a lot she could do about it except be constantly alert for any odd behavior on his part. Or hers.

Sophie jammed on her own Akubra hat and thanked the last fading stars of the night she'd worn sturdy walking boots, something she needed most places in the top end.

During the night they'd all managed to sleep in snatches after the emotional trauma of the day, and even Odette, apart from the indigestion and backache she normally suffered from, didn't seem any worse for the experiences of the day before.

'Your baby must be one tough little munchkin, Odette,' Sophie said as she finished her weak tea, courtesy of one teabag discovered at the bottom of her bag and shared between four cups.

'Tougher than his mother,' Odette said with a wobble in her voice. The young mum's eyes were heavily shadowed and her fingers stroked her belly as if to reassure herself and her baby that everything would be fine.

Sophie tamped down her own misgivings. Odette and her baby were the greatest worry. 'I think you're holding up amazingly well.' She tipped out the dregs and rinsed the cup before she slid her bag over her shoulder. 'We'll be as quick as we can. Your baby needs you to be calm. We've done the hard part and survived the landing.'

Smiley said, 'You'll have something to tell the grandchildren about in thirty years.'

'If I have grandchildren.'

'You've water and some food and a safe place. Make sure you stay hydrated; drink at least a bottle every hour. We're taking three bottles each and some chocolate. No matter what happens, don't leave this spot,' Sophie reminded her. 'Sighting of the crash site is still the most likely way for rescue. Lost in the bush is the easiest way to die.'

Odette scrubbed her eyes again and the mascara from yesterday was giving her a sad and sorry panda look. 'I'm not going anywhere. I wish I'd never left home.'

Sophie felt the loss of the woman who'd touched up her lipstick at the clinic only a few short days ago. 'I know. It's natural to worry about your baby. I'd like to think I'd do as well as you if I was in your position.'

Odette sniffed. 'You wouldn't cry like I do.'

Sophie hugged her and whispered, 'Didn't you see me yesterday after setting William's shoulder. I was a mess.'

Odette scrubbed her eyes with the back of her hand and peered at Sophie. 'Really? I didn't see that.'

'Good,' Sophie said and looked around to make sure none of the men had heard. 'But I felt better afterwards.'

'Thanks. It helps to know I'm not the only one to feel weepy.'

'I'm not that strong. Just on the outside.' Sophie glanced at her brother who was probably giving Levi some pointers as well. 'Look,' she said. 'This isn't going to happen, but if you do go into labor, stay cuddled up to Smiley. He'll look after you. Rest and remember you're designed to do it. Be calm and let it happen. Babies only need to be next to their mother. And remember first babies take a long time and we'll be back. Don't give up on us.'

Odette shook her head and her eyes filled again with tears. 'You shouldn't go. Levi shouldn't leave me.' She clutched at Sophie's arm. 'Neither of you should.'

Sophie drew the younger woman into her arms and hugged her. 'You'll be fine. We'll be back as quick as we can. But we need to walk out before it gets too hot.'

Odette started to cry and Sophie chewed her lip and glanced at Levi. She'd made everything worse.

Levi crossed to his sister and drew her into the circle of his arms. 'Shh, honey. One day away. That's all it'll take. You and William have a day on the land, relax and enjoy the scenery.'

Odette hiccoughed. 'Relax?' Her lip quivered as Levi handed her over to William to comfort. 'Please be careful,' Odette said to her brother.

He nodded. 'We'll be back for you in another chopper.'

'He'll fly back for you,' Sophie said dryly. 'I'll be cheering from home.'

Odette's lips tugged in an almost smile. 'Chicken.'

'We won't be long.' Levi knew how ridiculous that statement was. They were walking out into the desert.

Such a dilemma. He hated to leave Odette, and the thought of her going into labor out here without him made him break into a cold sweat.

Please God, don't let that happen.

He'd spent his life trying to keep her safe and he'd failed dismally. But he couldn't send Sophie off on her own even though he suspected she'd be tougher in the outback than him.

He did have faith in William, though he wasn't quite sure how that had happened. And they'd be as quick as they could, but there was no use waiting for a rescue that might never happen. They had to walk out.

They left without looking back and he felt like a deserter as he followed Sophie's back down a natural trail. Initially he tried to choose direction but his feet seemed to find the ground more uneven than Sophie did and eventually he fell in behind her because it was easier going. It felt strange to let another person lead, let alone a slip of a girl younger than him.

The rocks shifted under his feet as his ankles threatened to twist on the uneven path. It made sense if the whole place was the result of erosion but it made walking fraught for injury. When he thought about it they'd taken a lot for granted to head off into the hills.

He caught up with Sophie and walked beside her. 'I've just had a nasty thought. We're relying on William's memory of a nomad's camp, from a muster, that happened over a year ago?'

She glanced across at him. 'That's what we all decided on.'

He pushed aside a branch that reached across their path. 'What if the camp moved on, which I imagine is likely.'

She raised her eyebrows. 'We can hope the camp moved closer, then, and not further away.'

That was simple, he thought, wryly. 'I love the way your mind works.' He bent down and picked up a walking-stick-sized branch, tested it, and then used it to part the grass in front.

She grinned at him and he found himself grinning back. 'Optimism is the code of the Kimberley.'

Was this woman for real? 'Spare me, Pollyanna. You just made that up. Though it is catchy.'

'Yep. But you can't change what you can't change.' She glanced around as the first rays of light warned of sunrise. 'More likely a hunter will find us than we'll find him, anyway.'

He hadn't thought of that. 'Do they do that? Appear out of nowhere? I thought it was all in movies and fiction.'

She stopped and faced him. Said seriously, 'I do believe that the medicine man knows if someone who shouldn't be here is around. I'm hoping they find us sooner rather than later.'

The growing light allowed them to see the ground in front of them more clearly as the sun crept closer to rising. He'd be interested to see the pace she'd keep up when she could see properly. 'Can we do this? Walk out safely? In the daylight heat?'

She stopped and looked at him. 'We can be sensible, yes, and cut down the risks, but it's a big land under a bigger sun.' She glanced at the imminent sunrise. 'We should move faster while we can.'

The morning blurred into a fast-paced bushwalk. Sophie pointed out another Gubinge tree, and he began to see others now that he recognized them. She showed him the low growing, wide-leafed bush tomatoes, which looked more like brown raisins. 'But you have to eat the ripe ones. The green ones are toxic like green potatoes.'

She picked a few and offered him one. When he didn't look inspired she ate one herself and grimaced. 'They're talking about growing these commercially for a savory spice. They're pretty pungent but you never know when you'll need them.'

He was over bush tucker. It was pretty hard to be the protective male when she held all the cards. A very novel experience for a man who'd always been the one people came to for help. 'Have you ever been to Sydney?' he asked.

She didn't even look at him. 'No.'

'Maybe one day I'll show you my favorite restaurant. The chef is one of the top three in Australia.' He'd actually quite like that. 'You'd love the food.'

She looked at him as if he'd offered a space shuttle to the moon. 'You think?'

Clearly not on her wish list. She had to be good for his conceited soul. He laughed and followed her along another ridge that bordered a treeless plain he hoped they didn't have to cross, but she was heading in that direction. Assuming she knew where she was going.

Almost as if she heard his thoughts she paused. 'If we keep the sun on our right shoulder we should be heading north. There's a dry creek bed through the middle of the plain and maybe even a few of the pools will have water in them. We'll conserve what we have and try to make it to the next gorge and I'm expecting more water by midday. Then we'll rest.'

Unobtrusively he pulled his compass from his pocket and checked what she said. She was right! What did he expect? It was pretty different taking orders and not actually minding it.

Though, he hadn't minded his first-grade teacher either. Miss Tee was a honey and the first woman he'd ever fallen in love with. Probably because she liked to take them outside for games when they got bored with English, but he did remember her long, long legs. Though he conceded Sophie's legs were even better.

She walked with a loose-limbed gait, sure-footed in her lace-up leather boots and her knee length shorts that it seemed women wore here, and despite her determination to appear always in command, she couldn't hide her femininity. Her bottom still jiggled.

He realized how few women he'd seen since he'd been here, and they'd all been wearing those knee length shorts. Maybe that was why she looked so good. But he didn't think so. He had a feeling she'd look good on the Rue in Paris.

He caught her glancing at him and it made him smile more.

'What are you smiling at?'

He straightened his face. 'I've only seen four women since I arrived a week ago. And one of them is my sister.'

She flicked her brows up and down. 'Bet that's different to your usual day.' Was that sarcasm?

She had no idea what his life was like. The hours he worked. The impact of having to tell a patient he couldn't save their sight or the sight of their child - the main reason he'd been unable to get here sooner as he'd tried to clear a backlog of people who needed him desperately. How he'd started to think he'd never be able to make a dent in the need out there. 'Yeah well, it's hard running a playboy mansion.'

She stopped and faced him. 'You run a playboy mansion?'

That actually stung. Did she really think him that shallow? Nothing like his surgery full of people with visual nightmares. 'It was a joke.'

She brushed his comment away. 'Good. Don't worry. We get women here. When the tourist season properly starts the Gibb River Road really moves. Campers and off-road vehicles everywhere and the resorts fill up. You'll see plenty of ladies then, if you're still around.'

She started walking again and he nearly missed her final comment.

'Which you shouldn't be for someone passing through.'

She'd brought it up again. He didn't have the energy to go into why he didn't want to talk about work. 'Are you ever going to forgive me for that throwaway comment?'

She looked at him, innocently. 'Sure. Nothing to forgive. I just don't trust you.'

Be warned, he told himself. To her, he said, 'Nice.'

She ignored his comment and went back to their original conversation. 'The tourist season is only for six months, from April until the humidity comes back again in October, November. Most people move on because a person sweats heavily as soon as they step outside.'

He thought about what she said, wondered about the implications on the health resources from the influx of older travelers for such small amounts of health personnel, but if he commented he might end up embroiled in more lies. Better to leave well enough alone, which was a shame, because he valued her opinion.

They walked on for an hour without conversation or awkwardness. A sense of peace seeped into the whirling in his thoughts. Despite the last twelve hours he began to lose some of the tension he held. He couldn't remember the last time he'd been with a woman without feeling he had to fill the silence.

The scenery continued with little change now they were crossing more open ground, and to his untrained eye it looked very similar up ahead. He could see how people like him became lost. 'Tell me about the camp we're heading to?'

She paused and looked at him, as if bringing her thoughts to the present. 'The family tribe we're looking for are semi-nomadic most of the year. They've returned to the old ways and move with the food, so that means berries available, fattest kangaroos, and relying on predicting the weather.'

He glanced at the bare plains. 'Do they come into settlements often?'

'The young men muster when needed, for cash, and that's how Smiley knows about them. I haven't actually met this community, but they'd have met other nurses from other towns and I would know people they know.'

'It's a long way from Jabiru Town.'

'They travel. I've been meaning to reach out this way – for immunization and to let the women know I have a midwifery clinic now - so if we find them that will be a bonus.'

A bonus with their helicopter crash. He huffed a small laugh. Pleased he could accommodate. Her ability to find positives astounded him.

They walked until the mid-morning and with relief they entered the foothills of the next range and the little shade that offered.

Lucky he'd kept in shape. He was determined he wasn't going to ask for a rest, but he'd used most of his water, except for a little he kept in case she needed it. Not that he imagined she'd ask. But enough unusual things had happened to them over the last twenty-four hours he wasn't guaranteeing they wouldn't have more unusual events.

'Looks to be a subtropical pocket ahead, that's promising,' she said.

Within half an hour they'd moved from the grass of the plains to the spiral pandana trees of the semi-rainforest, and not much further on they found larger boulders and finally a small pool of algoid water.

The creek bed sloped up the gully and Sophie pointed to the narrowing gorge higher up. 'If we climb a little we'll find cleaner water, and it's probably worth the effort. We'll stay here for a couple of hours until the sun is well behind our backs.'

They both needed to rest, which would be hard with the idea of Odette still back at the wreck site, but Sophie was as aware of that as he.

'No problem.' Levi said. 'You said you'd find water. This place is amazing.' She was amazing. He looked around at the narrow strip of tropical foliage which seemed so out of place in the arid areas they'd just trekked through. There was a definite line where damp met dry and the rest of the gorge stretched away from them back to the plain of red dirt and spinifex.

He heaved himself up and around a few larger boulders and the subtle sound of running water gurgled more loudly.

'The flow must have disappeared into an underground creek because there's no flow further down,' she said.

He looked back and all he could see, water wise, was the green pool. He didn't have her skills of discernment, obviously.

One last steep-sided boulder, almost room-sized, stood between them and a ring of promising palm trees, but it was too high to step up onto.

He wedged himself between the gorge wall and the boulder and crab walked up the gap and was reminded of the indoor rock climbing he'd enjoyed in his youth. Crumbly rock grated against his arm as he heaved himself up. It felt good to do something physical apart from walking. When he craned his neck, the sky was decorated with a palm tree on an impossible angle that arched for the sun.

Then he was up. Not easy but worth it. The pool she'd promised lay in front of him. 'This is great,' he called down to her. The rocky pool lay fringed with ferns. Set deep in the gully under the fuzzy roots of an outstretched palm was a big bath-sized rock pool catching the water from above.

'The water's clean and deep.'

When he turned to offer his hand, he expected her to shimmy up with his support but she hesitated and turned her head to search for an alternative route, which was crazy when he knew this was the easiest. Reluctant to touch him? 'Not the time for being stubborn.'

His hand fell as he considered her refusal. There was a limit to independence. He'd thought they'd got over that in the walk. Some of his pleasure in the spot dissipated but he kept his voice matter of fact.

'I don't bite.' He held his hand out again. 'There's a nice pool up here. Why skin your knees when I can help you up?'

She brushed the hair from her face and looked at him, as if measuring the danger, and the skidding of her eyes confirmed it was the idea of contact that had her worried. He didn't get it.

'You're right,' she said. As if she'd already told herself the same. She took his hand and it was a beginning but he wasn't sure of what.

He lifted her easily, which helped his ego no end, until she was balanced on the rock beside him and could see the pool with the tiny waterfall at one end.

'Nice.' A small smile. 'Thanks.' She moved to the other side of the pool, well away from him.

They both looked at the water, he from his side and she from hers. Tiny fish flickered at the edge of the pond and the gurgle of the water over rocks from the waterfall dominated the sounds of the bush.

He crouched down and rinsed his water bottle before he drank deeply then refilled the one in his bag as well. She did the same and he looked across the small expanse of water at her bent head. He didn't get why she was so quiet. 'Is there something you're worried about or not telling me?'

'What?' Her voice faltered and then strengthened. She'd jumped. He saw it. She looked away from him.

'You mean apart from falling out of the sky? Or having to trek in the sun through a desert to get help?' She raised her eyebrows. 'No. Why should I be worried?'

He guessed her issues weren't for sharing then. 'Fine. I'll leave you in peace.' Stop trying to get her attention. The woman could make him edgy and awkward like a teenager and he didn't like the sensation. Or the fact he needed her to actually survive.

Lord it was hot. The pool looked good. Too good. 'We're staying here for a while, you said?'

'A couple of hours.'

'Then I'm in for a swim.' He undid his laces and slipped off his boots and socks. Bliss. He stretched and curled his toes. They'd covered some distance today.

Then he pulled his sticky shirt off and spread it on the rock beside him. Maybe the sun would take some of the sweat stink out of it. When he reached for his jeans she squeaked and he looked across.

Her eyes had widened. 'What are you doing?'

He stopped and looked around for a reason he shouldn't. 'A dip? I'm hot and bothered and it looks good. You said pools were safe.' He raised his eyebrows. 'Is there a problem?'

'Only if you take much more off.' She looked away. 'I'm not used to men stripping in front of me.'

Stripping? He huffed at himself. He guessed he was. 'Not a nudist. I'll stop in time.'

No one had ever complained about his body before. He slid his shorts down and stepped out of them. His boxers were black and perfectly discreet.

He balanced on the uneven stones at the edge of the pool and tried to work out the least painful way to enter the water. He realized he had his belly sucked in and almost blew it by laughing out loud. She wouldn't be looking anyway.

'These rocks are nasty on bare feet.' In fact they hurt like hell as he tried to ease into the water without damage to his toes. The rocks shifted and sliced at him as if they were intent on unbalancing him.

He'd have to describe the smile she gave him as evil. 'Yes, aren't they?' She sat without making any move to undress.

She had to be as hot as he was. 'You coming in?'

'I'll see if anything bites you first.' Her voice deadpan so he had no idea if she was serious or not.

Nice. 'What happened to the appreciative passenger who thanked me for landing the chopper?'

Chapter 7

Sophie fought panic. All of a sudden she was fighting to keep distance from him and it was getting harder and harder. She wasn't sure when it happened. Just little moments from after the crash when he'd given her that extra bit of support.

Saw her distress at helping Smiley. Held her shirt. That embrace.

Or this morning when he never complained once though she knew he was hot and dry, and she had to keep reminding herself he was from the city and wasn't used to their headlong scramble over the plains and gorges. He probably worked out on some treadmill in a swanky gym for hours but still, this morning had been tough.

But the big moment had been when he'd suggested she take his hand – had lifted her effortlessly, strong arms and shoulders holding her safe and easily. Sinewy ripples of muscle in his shoulders through his shirt and strong determined thighs in his jeans as he pulled her up and made sure she was stable.

Not fair.

How was a girl supposed to keep her head when he looked so darn strong and confident and she was tired and starting to doubt that she would be able to find the tribe and shouldn't have agreed to leave Odette in case she birthed with just Smiley there. And when he'd reached down with those big, capable hands, when he was supposed to be city soft and reliant on her, she knew if she let him she'd just sail to the top of the rock with no effort.

That was when she'd got really scared. When she'd started to realize he was occupying too much of her mind space. In fact nearly all of her mind, as she blanked out the horror of the last twenty-four hours and the fear that she'd made some dangerously bad decisions.

That sort of thing would make you think of mortality, with the good things of life she'd like to taste before the end. But this wasn't the end, she reminded herself forcefully. This was just a scary interlude and they would get help.

Odette would be fine and Levi and his sister would fly away back to Sydney in a few days and everyone in the Kimberley would forget them.

Even Sophie Sullivan. And they would forget her. Fast.

Levi's voice broke into her thoughts. 'I said, nothing bit me, are you coming in?'

She wouldn't mind but it was a very small pool. 'I don't know. It looks cold from up here.'

Levi floated on his back, which gave her too good a view of his chest and shoulders. She swallowed. She'd known it. Levi without his shirt was a bad thing.

'Deliciously cool and I feel one hundred percent better than I did before I got in,' he said lazily.

His hair was plastered to his head and droplets ran down his strong chin and dripped onto his chest and she couldn't help comparing him to Brad. Poor Brad.

Levi had corded bulk and the ripples and dips of his abdomen made even Smiley look like a kid. Her own belly knotted and she looked away. She'd never seen such a discreetly muscular man in her life and no matter how much she tried to lie to herself, the darn man was powerfully attractive.

But it was hot. And she was tired. If she got in, she could float with her face away from him. Sitting out here, it would look silly for her to turn her back now. Not like she hadn't already shown everyone her bra when she'd volunteered to use her shirt for Smiley's sling.

'Turn around, then.'

She waited until his water-slicked shoulders teased her again before hurriedly stripping off her boots, socks and shorts. She draped her shirt close to the edge where she could reach it as soon as she left the water.

She eased herself down on her bottom. She'd been bruised before by the piled rocks getting into pools, and local knowledge suggested to slide in from a low height. The bottom of the pool would only be waist height if she were to stand but deep enough to hide under and, as she slid deeper, oh so cool and wonderful after the distance they'd walked in the heat this morning.

'Ohh, yes.' She sighed her pleasure as the water eddied up her legs and thighs with delicious coolness. Her breath sucked in as the water passed her stomach and breasts, with a final shiver as she submerged her shoulders until only her nose and eyes were showing.

Ha. Not much for him to look at now.

She slid her head beneath the surface, letting the coolness cover and calm her. She surfaced her mouth again, enough to say, 'I'm in,' and then sank bank to nose level.

'You sure you can breathe?' His eyes laughed at her and his mouth curved in that wicked smile she'd known would be lethal. Why not pull that one out of his arsenal? Damn him.

'What happens if I make a wave?' He crossed his hands and threatened to ripple the water and sink her.

She tried to imagine him as a scrubby toddler, as Odette's teasing brother, as anything but the hunk across from her. She pulled her mouth out of the water. 'Some boys never grow up. I bet you were the head of the pack at school. One of those boys who tell everyone else what to do.'

They'd floated quite close now, she on her front using her hands along the bottom in the shallow places to drift around the pool. The brilliant idea of maintaining distance and turning her back had been forgotten as she waited, surprisingly intrigued for his answer.

A shadow passed his face. 'Being at the top of the pile is much more comfortable than being on the bottom. But I'm not a bully.'

She sniffed and paddled some more. 'That's what all bullies say.'

He shook his head. 'My father bullied my mother, even into another baby when she wasn't well enough to have one. Odette. She died. Cardiac problems. My grandfather, a very rich man who didn't need to be grasping, was not a nice person either, so maybe he got it from there.'

A tantalizing glimpse at the life of Levi the child was not something she'd expected and it touched a maternal instinct bone she didn't know she had. And didn't need.

Please don't tell me more. She didn't want to know. Really she didn't.

A wild budgerigar, bright green and busy, hopped with his mate and chattered in a tree above their heads, and she gazed up at it trying to form the sentence to change the subject. 'Did he make life hard for you?' Not the words she intended. At all.

'Not me. I spent most of my younger years in boarding school. I wasn't there enough to be harmed by my father. I had an older brother who bore the brunt in holidays. Kyle took after my mother. Kind and quiet, one of life's gentle men, he shielded me. He confirmed the difference between good and bad behavior and humility and posturing. I'm eternally grateful to him for that.'

'You said "had"?'

He looked through her. 'He died when I was thirteen. He had macular degeneration, went blind, then stepped out in front of a truck. My father said Kyle knew the truck was coming. I called him a liar.' He fingered the scar on his chin.

Sophie wanted to reach out and comfort him. 'What do you say?'

He focused on her face. 'Never. Kyle hated being blind but he loved us too much to think of leaving us alone.'

She could easily imagine a young boy losing his big brother after losing his mother.

'I took over the protector role and made sure Odette was never worried by him.' He rubbed the scar again and she suspected the origin. No wonder he worried about Odette. He'd feel he had to do for her what Kyle had done for him.

'That's a terrible tragedy for your family to go through.'

'Even the strongest of us are shaped by events in our childhood.' He shook the droplets of water from his hair as if to shake off the past. 'What about you? There's just you and William?'

She sank back further in the water, loosening her neck as she realized she'd tensed her shoulders while he'd shared his past. 'Just Smiley and me. Our parents died four years ago, truck accident, so I guess we were lucky we weren't children. Smiley's easy to live with and we both have work we love.'

'Smiley. Great name.'

A vision of her brother, tall and serious, with just a twinkle in his eye to let her know he found something she'd said amusing, was the one solid thing in her life. The one person she could trust. But she couldn't quiet that voice that said there were facets in Levi that appealed to her, and not just the external ones, and maybe she could learn to trust him too.

He floated to the edge of the pool and rested his back against a flat rock while he considered her. 'Who let you down and broke your heart?'

Just when she thought she might trust him. 'What makes you think my heart's been broken?'

He ignored that question to ask, 'Someone in Perth?'

She never talked about it. Smiley hadn't asked. Her friend Kate had a new baby on the way and was immersed in her new husband. Kate didn't need Sophie's baggage. She'd come back from Perth and buried the lot.

Suddenly it was easy to unearth that past. To talk. 'Some guy I worked with.' Was he really interested in this? She glanced across at him and then away. Something in his face told her he hadn't asked her lightly. That he genuinely wanted to understand and she guessed it would help explain why she was the way she was.

The picture of Brad in her mind wasn't quite as sharp as it had been. A good thing. 'He was the head of Obstetrics in my training hospital, actually. Born in Australia, but his parents were wealthy immigrants. He never talked about where their money came from. I guess he grew up with different values than I did.'

'In what way?' He asked the question quietly, not demanding. If she didn't want to answer she didn't have to, but maybe she needed to clarify what went wrong in her own mind.

'The way he treated people.' Yep, that was what she'd disliked the most. 'Like they were servants under his feet. He wanted old money joined with his new wealth. I kept telling him I had no money, but he was so impressed that my great, great grandfather was one of the first settlers in Western Australia. Kept telling people when he introduced me that I had a history his family didn't have. Had this funny idea that because two generations ago my great grandfather opened up the Kimberley it made me almost outback royalty.'

'Princess Sophie,' he teased.

'Yeah, right. Not a lot of call for a crown out here in the heat and the dust.'

He shredded a leaf while he listened. 'What attracted you to him?'

She looked past Levi into the fronds behind him. 'The usual, I guess. Not that I'd actually fallen for anyone like him before. He was good looking, quite powerful, and in the beginning he wanted to do the things I really enjoyed. He courted me the old-fashioned way, and I liked that.' She avoided his eyes. 'I'm not a person who is easy with casual sex.'

'I'd never have guessed.'

She looked up to see him smile. She'd swear he was laughing at her but it was strangely liberating to say the things she hadn't said out loud before. She pulled a face. 'And you're a smart Alec.'

He held his hands up. 'I'm sorry. Couldn't resist.'

'Sure you couldn't.'

After a moment the mood shifted back to serious when he asked, 'What happened?'

She couldn't believe she was talking about this. 'He changed. Oh, he started off doing the things I wanted to do. Walks, sailing, museums, but really he wanted great restaurants, opening night shows, to be seen. To show me off on his arm.'

'I've met men like that,' he said. 'And women.'

'Don't get me wrong, that was nice too, but when I agreed to marry him... that's when everything changed.'

'In what way?'

'I became his property. As if he lost respect for me as an individual. As a person.' She looked away. Didn't say, he demanded the sex I hadn't felt ready for. 'He bought clothes for me. Pushed me to sign the prenuptial agreement. Checked my jewelry and shoes and handbag and made sure I had it all coordinated. Like one of those cartoon snowballs that kept getting bigger and faster, until he began to talk about me giving up my job. Started this campaign of speak when spoken to.'

'That must have been hard.' He sounded serious but she saw the twinkle in his eyes and knew he was suppressing a smile.

Funnily enough it didn't bother her. In fact it had the opposite effect. Her own lips twitched. 'My word it was.'

Levi whistled. 'That's a few rules.'

'Tell me about it.'

Then Levi asked, 'Did you love him?'

'I thought I did.' Would have sworn it when they became engaged, but now she really didn't know. She could see how the unease that had grown enormous toward the end of their relationship had been there from the beginning.

'I must have because I put up with my reservations. Then he began keeping track of where I was. Who I was with.'

'Stalking?'

'Looking back? Yes. I'd say that's an accurate description.'

'Then I'd say you did well to get out when you did.'

Not a nice man for Sophie. Levi knew those kind of men. Image being all important, and their women had to be aware of the rules. Rules that didn't apply to the men.

He asked the hard one. 'And was he faithful?'

'I thought so.' She looked away. 'I was a fool.'

Levi saw the flash of hurt. The fact that she went on said a lot for her strength and honesty and he had a sudden desire to meet and deal with the jerk for her. And to comfort Sophie.

'He'd been sleeping with his secretary the whole time. Everyone knew.'

'Except you.'

She nodded and cast her gaze around the pebble-lined hollow they lay in. 'He told more lies than the rocks in this pool.' She shook her head in disbelief, perhaps at the lies. Perhaps at herself for falling into his deceit. 'Apparently it'd been going on for years but he never offered to marry her.'

Levi said nothing. What was there to say? Other than offer to track him down and let him know what a prize creep he was.

Sophie glared at a bird that caught her eye but he knew she wasn't seeing it. 'What offended me the most was his part-time girlfriend wasn't good enough to marry, only to sleep with. Creep.'

'What did you do?' Something that hurt, he hoped.

'I sold his ring and donated the money to the maternity unit for an expensive water birth renovation so he'd have to see what he bought.'

Levi laughed. 'Perfect.'

She smiled but her eyes were still distant. 'Then I came home. To Smiley. Got on with my life in a place where people say what they mean and don't cheat.'

'I'm sorry you trusted such a man.'

'Thank you. And sadly—' she smiled but there was no humor in her eyes '—I have a chip on my shoulder about wealthy doctors who lie.'

Levi looked away and winced. Well then, he was screwed.

Sophie closed her eyes. Why on earth had she told him all that and made herself vulnerable again? She should learn the fine skill of shutting up.

It had been a dismal time, back then. Best to change the subject.

'Home was good,' she continued, because it seemed she couldn't shut up. 'My brother never said a thing. Except "shortest engagement in history". He's so deadpan most of the time you never know what's going on in his head, though apparently your sister can read him. I've never seen him as animated as the other night at Xanadu.'

Levi shrugged but there was a tiny frown between his eyes. 'Odette likes him a lot.'

'I don't think you could get two people more dissimilar in up-bringing.' Her forehead wrinkled despite a conscious effort to remain impassive.

At least Levi recognized her misgivings and maybe had a few of his own. Good. Smiley and Odette would never work.

Levi shook his head. 'Before she met the father of her baby I'd have agreed with you. That's my greatest regret so far, that I didn't keep her safe from men like him. Tom was a dangerous and malicious opportunist and no loss to his unborn child I'm afraid. I think your brother is restoring Odette's faith in chivalrous men.' He grinned. 'And she's very pregnant. No harm can be done.'

Chivalrous. Such an old-fashioned word but in this context, the perfect description of Smiley.

'Are you chivalrous?' It popped out like a bubble from the waterfall and subtly the mood in the pool changed.

'I used to be. Before I became tired and jaded.' Then very softly, 'For you I could be.'

She watched that curve to his lips that she was finally seeing more often. She could feel the brush of his gaze as he tilted his head and smiled with that devilish curve to his mouth. 'Open doors. My cloak across a muddy puddle. I'd enjoy it.'

The notion warmed and alarmed her. Time to break back to the previous mood, she thought, with a little spurt of panic. 'What made you tired and jaded?'

The smile straightened and disappeared. 'Someone died. Two years ago, now. In a way that affected how I thought about my achievements. I've been running on the treadmill since, but I won't bore you with it.'

Boring me might be safer, she thought, but she didn't say it. Couldn't make the effort to turn the tide of awareness she'd begun to drift in.

He floated across the pool and closed in on her like a silent, smiling merman. His eyes darker and his lips parted as if he might whisper something – or do something else...

'I must admit,' his voice very quiet, 'I feel more alive than I have in a long time.'

He felt alive, did he? She felt butterflies and the tingle of gooseflesh along her shoulders and arms. She should move away but her body felt so heavy in the water. She hung suspended.

'Might be something to do with the fact we nearly died yesterday.' Now her voice sounded breathy and unsure. It felt as though they were the only two people in the world and even the coolness of the water temperature faded.

'No doubt.' He sank under the water to his chin until not just his strong, brown shoulders were under the water but his neck and throat as well. Just his laughing grey eyes above his nose and mouth but they were shadowed by the overhanging palms that darkened the planes of his cheeks. 'It's good to be alive.'

With his words a leaf spun across the water towards her. The leaf twisted and bumped against her chin. It was just a leaf, but she could feel her heart thundering under the water. His gaze locked with hers, and it was as if he blew air over her skin. Ridiculous. She was under the water for goodness sake.

Yet here she was with tiny flutters of heated awareness in a cold pond of sudden desire. It shouldn't have been erotic... but it was. A stranger, in a strange place, and strange feelings she hadn't experienced before. Enough to kick in her belly and make her aware of the fullness in her breasts and the beat of her heart.

Then his breath rippled across the water to tickle her face. She moistened her lips to say something inane but before she could form the words he'd drifted closer until their noses touched with a little bump, like two leaves in a deserted pond, and she held still.

All the time he stared into her eyes and she could do little but breathe in and out and stare back and wonder at the dozen different blue rings inside his grey eyes and those dark, dark lashes drawing her closer. She knew he was going to kiss her. Should be backing but was drawn towards him by the primitive pull she had no control over.

When his lips finally touched hers, they brushed, slow and gentle, an open-mouthed whisper of lips that impacted like an earth tremor against hers. Her lids drooped as she breathed in. His mouth pressed more firmly, darting electrical tremors down her arms and legs that sent waves of mingled breath and kicks of desire back up into her chest.

The sensations expanded in seismic rings of awareness and lust, and suddenly it was closer she needed to be not further away.

Then he took her mouth, melded and meshed their souls in this primitive place a day after they'd nearly died. Somehow, with that potent kiss, he touched the part of her that no-one had ever touched... and she was his. That simple and that complicated.

They came together, in the pond, immersed in sensation as his hands slid from her shoulder down past her waist until he cupped both hips and pulled her toward him and, somehow, her fingers became entangled in his thick hair and luxuriated in the springiness beneath her fingers as her breasts squashed against his chest.

Time passed, their mouths learning the other, moment by glorious moment, and she slipped deeper and deeper under his spell until she realized she was clutching at him as he tried to pull back.

She opened her eyes, focused, and stilled. Oh my. Did she never learn? She pulled herself away and would have moved further if he hadn't put his hand out and stilled her.

'It's okay. It's just a kiss. You're so beautiful,' he said, his voice heavy and deep and she shuddered another breath as he lifted a strand of hair off her forehead.

He pulled back. Floated away. And left her bereft.

The blood pounded in her ears and she watched him, like a rabbit in headlights, mesmerized as he increased the distance between their bodies. Gradually she began to feel the world again and with it the sounds of the birds overhead and the wind in the leaves and the thunder of her heart.

The silence between them was broken only by the noisy budgerigar and his mate. Levi floated with his back to her while she climbed out, carefully, so as not to hurt her feet.

Sophie's hands shook, were stupidly clumsy as she wiped herself over with her shorts, and her lower limbs still wobbled as she redressed damply. Still in a daze from one kiss. A mouth-tingling caress like nothing she'd ever experienced before.

Brad had been practiced, smooth, and now she could see one-dimensional – not like Levi. The man was a city marauder of devastating understatement and finesse. A gift and homage to her as opposed to a conquering taker.

She shivered, not with cold, but with a new knowledge of greater danger. Where was the line between attraction and wanting to be lost in a man's arms or the terrible danger of falling in love? She knew how much pain that could cause.

Her damp shirt stuck to her bra and outlined her nipples and she pulled the material out from her body to air it. It would dry all too quickly when they crossed the next plain but it embarrassed her horribly at this moment. She settled herself facing the gorge they'd climbed and breathed slowly and carefully to regain her composure. She could do that.

Couldn't look to the pool and Levi. Her lips thrummed like she'd just eaten a Kakadu plum. When in fact she'd tasted something much better.

The water splashed behind her and a muffled curse forced a reluctant smile. He'd stubbed his toe. Good. Take his mind off kissing her.

She dug in her bag and pulled out the chocolate bar. It bent in her hand, soft and squishy and she looked at it with a sigh. His would be the same.

Hot chocolate was good in winter, and even like this when you hadn't had anything to eat since a tart piece of fruit. Something to take her mind off other parts of her body. The paper ripped in her teeth and the first sweet taste oozed onto her tongue.

She sucked the wrapper as she considered their options. Anything not to think of the pool and what had passed between them. They'd cross the plain in the afternoon sun and hopefully find the camp before dark.

That was the scary part.

Because if they didn't...

Chapter 8

Levi had had to force himself away. God she was beautiful. And luscious. And he wanted her. There was no doubt about that but what the hell was he doing? There was no future in this, just heartbreak for Sophie and maybe even for him.

It was bloody lucky this pool was cold, which would help, but even then he'd have to stay submerged till he had himself under control. He'd nearly lost himself. Another minute and they'd have passed the point of no return, and she was too innocent and trusting to realize.

He guessed he wasn't chivalrous at all.

He fisted his hands under the water and forced himself to calm. What had he been thinking?

Fool. He hadn't been thinking. He'd been feeling. Feeling the attraction that had slammed him the first time he saw her. Indulging in a daydream, or more like an erotic fantasy to play nymphs and satyrs in an oasis.

How low could he go?

Not a great way to say thank you to the woman trying to save them all.

But she'd looked so kissable with her satin skin and fine-boned shoulders that made him ache like he hadn't ached for years. If he were honest, he'd wanted to kiss her since the night she'd come to Xanadu. To be more honest, he'd wanted to do more than kiss and he'd very nearly had his way.

She would have hated him.

He would have hated himself.

He would have deserved all the loathing.

By three they were on their way again and neither mentioned the kiss in the pool. The heat bit into Levi's shoulders through his shirt and the grass crunched dryly beneath their feet. The plain stretched ahead of them in a seemingly endless roll with stunted trees and anthills their only shade.

Levi could feel the difference; the awareness between them had increased, the air vibrated and not just with heat from the sun. He'd caused this. Created her distress. He could regret instigating the kiss but not the kiss itself because there was something about that moment that said it had to be.

But his stupid lack of control had caused Sophie embarrassment and he regretted that deeply. He needed to find some way to lighten the strain between them. 'Sophie?'

She jumped when he spoke. He wished she wouldn't do that. Not for the first time he wondered about the man who had caused her to do that.

She stopped until he caught up and walked with her. 'Can you tell me about the anthills? How they're made?'

'Termite mounds. Not anthills.'

He looked again. 'Okay. Termite mounds, then.' Everywhere, from small bumps in the dirt to huge towers taller than a man. Even on the cliff faces when he looked.

More interesting than he expected. 'Can you tell me about termites?'

She stopped again and put her hands on her hips. 'What makes you think I know?'

She had an endearing pose. Endearing everything. Lots of endearing to be had. 'You know all.'

Her eyes narrowed. 'You are so full of—'

'Ah, ah, ah.' He shook his finger as he cut her off. 'Are you saying you don't know?'

She sighed. 'Termites are blind.'

She may pretend resignation but he saw the easing of tension in her and it made him feel good about himself. Strange. And a reprieve from feeling bad.

'Termites are opaque and the workers can live for thirty years.' She gave him a tentative smile. 'The queen can even live up to eighty years.'

He smiled back. 'That'd be right. Poor man doing all the work.' He gestured to the two-metre, 6 foot high tower of dirt. 'What are the mounds made of?'

She rolled her eyes at him. 'Mounds are made with saliva, spinifex, mud, termite poo, and they grow at a rate of about thirty centimetres, or about a foot, every ten years.' She pointed to a mound that had split. 'You can tell when they're abandoned because an active mound that's broken is repaired very quickly.'

He smiled at the way she loved to share her knowledge. It was one of those little things he'd grown to recognize and like about her. The passion for her world.

He hadn't exhibited a lot of passion lately. The joy and achievement had gone and he was beginning to see why his friends had been worried. When he went back he needed to search out the reasons and find the love for his work.

He patted the huge mound they were passing. 'There's a lot of years here.'

She paused and looked around with that love of her surroundings shining from her eyes. 'The story of the Kimberley is all about lots of years. This whole area is the product of erosion of a giant mountain range, The Leopold, millions of years ago. That's why the ground's so rocky and bare.'

And why not much grew around here, he guessed. 'So no bushrangers right out here in the past?'

'Not bushrangers, but there is a story…' She smiled and he knew they'd recovered some of their rapport.

'Yes?'

'An escapee from the law was tracked out here and he ambushed one of the policemen and stuffed the body inside a termite mound.'

'Did they find the body?'

'The termites repaired the mound, the man confessed years later, but the remains were never found.'

The woman was a mine of scary information.

'You got it.'

She made him smile. Often, most of the time. Even through this disaster. 'So, I'd better not annoy you?'

She showed her teeth. 'Or you'll never be found.'

Sophie had sealed what had happened between them at the pool like the termites sealed their mounds, but she still felt embarrassed that she'd let him kiss her. She didn't have the headspace for the questions that had arisen from that kiss. She was focused now on getting home. Desperately.

She was doubly glad of his environmental interest because she could feel the fear build as the day lengthened. She'd been fairly confident this morning, and still sure they would find the camp at lunch, but this afternoon her water bottle grew emptier and conversation between them dried up like the sweat on their bodies, and she began to consider their options.

She must have sighed because he looked across at her and touched her shoulder. 'What's wrong?

She stopped and unconsciously her hand came over the top of his for comfort. 'It's taking longer than I'd hoped.'

He turned her into his chest and moved so she was out of the sun behind his body - a different type of embrace than the last one she didn't want to think about - and she rested her forehead on him for a moment. His voice rumbled in his chest. 'We'll find them, if not today, then tomorrow. If we don't, we know we can make it back to the others.'

Could they? She thought about how far they'd walked. Yes, they could. She could almost feel the strength transferring from him to her. His confidence boosted hers, probably unjustifiably, not that she wanted him to tell her otherwise. She had enough doubts for both of them.

Her stomach growled. 'I don't know about you but I'm getting hungry,' she mumbled into his shirt.

'Where's a drive-through Gubinge tree when you want one?' He kicked the ground. 'There's always the grubs. Ten fat ones a day did you say?'

She had to laugh. Or she'd cry. But she did feel better. Then he put her away from him and dug in his pocket. He held up his liquid chocolate bar. 'I was saving this one for you.'

She shook her head vehemently. 'I'm not eating your chocolate.'

'Sure you are.' He pointed to the hills up ahead. 'We'll stop there and fight about it.' Then he patted her hair and took her pack from her back and captured her fingers. 'Let's go.'

He pulled her fingers gently, and suddenly the strength came back along with her focus and she walked beside him with their hands swinging together over the red earth. She didn't know when it happened but suddenly she did trust him. Was happy to allow him to shoulder some of the burden, something so out of character for her she didn't understand how he'd achieved it. Especially after the kiss. Or was it because of the kiss?

Maybe she did see traits in Levi that she hadn't seen in any man she'd been drawn too. Good traits. Kind traits. That brought her respite from the tension they were living through.

They were close to the last foothills when the Aboriginal elder appeared. His wizened skin crinkled in mahogany folds and his grey hair hung long and straggled. He stood beside a termite hill, carrying a spear for hunting and little else.

Levi stopped suddenly but Sophie kept going. 'He wants us to follow him.'

Levi glanced across at her. 'Guess you were right again.'

Sophie sighed with relief. Not before time. They were running out of afternoon. She'd done one thing right then. 'This was a good one to win.'

The elder took them to a side gully and presented them with another fresh pool to drink and cool themselves. He didn't speak and she watched Levi, with hidden amusement, as he attempted to sign their story but the old man just stared at him.

'I doubt he's learnt English for the little use he'd have for it.' She handed him a stick. 'Maybe if you drew a picture in the sand?'

Levi's sand helicopter left a lot to be desired but a broad grin from the elder seemed as though he'd figured where they'd come from. Levi drew four people and then pointed to himself and Sophie, indicating the other two were still at the helicopter.

The old man nodded, seriously, and pointed to the sun and then an arc in the sky to almost sunset, and gestured they follow him, and that they'd be able to get back to the others after that.

Sophie didn't know if it was her imagination, or just the relief, but the walking was less strenuous, more shaded, and yet seemed as though they covered more ground.

An hour before sunset they came to the camp, a collection of half a dozen lean-tos, with several brown eyed, brown-skinned toddlers scuffling in the dust.

It was unusually quiet and a quorum of women had congregated around a lean-to at the end of the camp. The hair on Sophie's arms stood up. Something was wrong. She glanced at Levi who raised his brows and shrugged. He could sense it too.

The oldest lady pointed to her. Sophie approached them diffidently, used to not catching the elder's eyes. The lady, probably the grandmother, pointed her finger at Sophie. 'You that nurse-sheila, eh?' She gestured into the lean-to with her head.

Trepidation swamped her and Sophie forced her head to lift as she glanced back at Levi. It seemed this day had more in store for her. Lord knew what she'd find but it seemed she would soon find out.

He took a step to follow her. 'Do you want me to come with you?' But the old lady gestured him away.

Sophie sighed. 'Nice thought but it's not going to happen. I'd say it's secret women's business.'

Sophie bent and followed the woman inside, and her heart bumped at the thought of the unknown and what may be expected of her. The air within the lean-to was stifling. The place seemed full of aunties and the grandmother, and the young girl who lay on the dry grass bed looked more like a frightened rabbit than a woman about to give birth.

'Oh Lord,' Sophie muttered. The sight of one tiny, very still and blue baby's foot resting between the mother's legs was enough to make Sophie feel like a frightened rabbit, too.

Was she too late to help?

A footling breech, so that didn't mean mother was definitely ready to push as a small foot could slip through a partially open cervix, but Sophie could hope. Either way baby's legs would come out before the head. If it all went well.

'And it will go well,' she said out loud, to bolster her own conviction. The women spoke back to her in a language where Sophie barely recognised the occasional word. There wouldn't be much conversation.

A caesarean section would have been a nice option to have in the wings in case of complications, Sophie wished fruitlessly, but that wasn't going to happen. All she could think of was the mantra from her training, hands off the breech, and hope the young mum had the energy to push when the time came.

The little foot twitched. Moved. Toes curled.

Sophie sucked in a breath of delighted relief. The baby was alive. Her day had improved enormously.

Now wasn't the time to ask why the girl wasn't near a hospital if she was close to birth time. Sophie knew that sometimes the fear of being away from their families made the young community women hide their pregnancies so they weren't sent away. But Sophie also knew the girl would be in trouble with the elders later for breaking the rules.

She knelt down and tried for a smile, then tapped her own chest. 'Sophie.'

The older lady pointed to the girl. 'Pearl.'

'Hello, Pearl,' Sophie said, but Pearl's frightened brown eyes skittered to the gaggle of aunties and refused to return. Sophie gestured for permission to feel the mother's abdomen and grandmother shooed her onto to the task as if to say hurry up.

Pearl's baby felt small, less than three kilos, which could be a good thing, or perhaps just felt small because it was breech and a lot of the baby had shifted down already into the pelvis. Pearl herself was fine-boned with no extra weight and Sophie would love to have known how long the labor had been going on.

'Long time like this?' she asked the grandmother. Hoping she would understand. Sophie suspected grandmother's English was way better than her own knowledge of this tribal language. There were so many dialects and this wasn't one she had skill in.

'Not long. We send to next station. They phone to get plane.'

Thank you, Grandmother.

'Good.' Sophie nodded and the weight on her shoulders lessened. At least someone was coming... eventually. And that would help Odette and Smiley too because they could pass the word and send help.

The next contraction arrived and Pearl whimpered with the pain but grunted with expulsive effort. Her baby's little foot descended another inch into the world and Sophie began to hope this would progress in a straightforward way.

At this moment there wasn't much Sophie could do except be there for the end. She couldn't listen to the baby's heartbeats because she didn't have any form of stethoscope, she didn't have gloves, or even the means to wash her hands, but she couldn't leave Pearl alone either.

Levi's support was denied because culturally Pearl's birthing was women's business and men were banned. Though, if she had a problem when the baby arrived, Sophie knew darn well she'd be yelling for Levi.

Just knowing he was there gave immense reassurance. She'd expect Levi's first aid skills and common sense meant solid help if she needed it.

Even if the Royal Flying Doctor Service aircraft was coming, help might not arrive before it was all over.

There was nothing to be done but settle herself more comfortably on the dusty floor and try to ignore the trickle of perspiration that ran down between her shoulder blades. She licked her lips and tasted the dryness of her mouth. A drink would have been good.

She mimed a drink and the grandmother sent one of the other aunties out to oblige. Sophie could use half to wash her hands.

All they could do was pray for a rapid second stage of labor but there was only so much praying she could do. She glanced around for something positive to focus on and her gaze rested on a brown shawl she could dry the baby with when it was born. That was a positive thought. When it was born.

The aunties all looked at her as if she should do something and she tried to block out the thoughts that didn't help. Thoughts about drugs, and oxygen, and pediatricians who may as well be on the moon. Hopefully the baby had grown well and wasn't too premature.

If the young mum had had no antenatal care then she was probably anemic to start with which increased her chance of bleeding afterwards, and any blood loss would make her dangerously depleted in red blood cells.

But there wasn't a lot Sophie could do about that either. She could rub mum's tummy to encourage clamping down of the uterus when the placenta was delivered and she could put the baby to the breast as soon as possible to release the natural hormones that were there to do the same thing.

Women had been birthing for thousands of years in the camps, she reassured herself, well before twentieth century medicine had decreed they were safer at the hospitals. Trouble was, now the elder women had begun to lose their skills as attendants, like any medical professional would, over the last hundred years.

She needed to think of more positives. At least the heat would make it unlikely for the baby to get cold, which breech babies tended to do as their body waited for the head to be born.

For some reason she thought of Levi's Pollyanna comment, and it steadied her because there was nothing wrong with looking on the bright side of things.

Pearl moaned again and this time baby's ankle came down almost to the knee and suddenly there was a second foot. So, fully dilated with progress. Best-case scenario.

'You're doing great, Pearl.' Sophie plastered a happy face on and nodded her head at the frightened girl and her attendants. The least she could do was be supportive instead of a harbinger of doom.

If the cervix was not fully opened then Pearl was going to push against it anyway. If she sat up it would be easier for baby and put more even pressure on the cervix. Sophie looked at the grandmother and gestured that they help Pearl to squat in a supported position.

She rolled her hands as if making speed. Gravity would help bring the baby down and hopefully all would happen quickly before the baby's cord became too squashed by the aftercoming head.

With Pearl upright her labor did seem to progress more quickly, first baby's knees and the thighs appeared with just the change of position and then Pearl pushed until a swollen black scrotum appeared and the women broke into voluble noise and exclamations at the evidence of a new male for the family.

The elder woman gestured to Sophie to grab the baby but Sophie shook her head emphatically.

She made a no gesture. And then a prayer one. Please.

This was where "hands off the breech" was most important. Sophie knew the natural curves of the mother's pelvis shaped the baby into his chin tucked into his chest and the arms by his side. If they pulled the baby downwards, his head would tip back into a bigger diameter and his arms might drag behind his head to create a complication that should never have happened.

'Please. No touch,' Sophie said and waved her hands in a negative sign. 'Baby knows.'

Little skinny buttocks were followed by hips, back and umbilical cord all came through next, and Sophie resisted the urge to feel the cord and count the heartrate of the baby.

She'd bet it was slower than her own thumping heart, but the less she touched, the less spasm the cord would endure.

There certainly wasn't anything else Sophie could do except prevent people pulling on the baby as he descended. She'd just ensure Pearl's baby came out with the back facing Sophie, so his head could lift from his chin-on- chest position to birth, just like a head-first baby did.

Grandmother clutched her hair and moaned and gestured to Sophie at the paleness of the baby and Sophie could tell she wanted to help make the baby come quicker. 'Soon,' Sophie soothed. 'All over soon.'

Sophie slipped her wrist between the baby's legs when the chest was through and first one shoulder and then the other was born so that baby was hanging all out with only the neck and head to come. Sophie's heart was thumping so loud in her ears she didn't doubt the aunties could hear but she was strangely calm.

She allowed the weight of the baby to hang a little to ensure the head stayed deflexed until the last moment and Sophie's bent legs ached from squatting almost under Pearl.

Now. Time to deliver the head. With one hand on top of the baby's shoulders and back of the neck and the other underneath on the baby's cheeks so when the head birthed it didn't spring out suddenly. The hardest part.

Baby's head had been rushed through the pelvis. To ease a baby slowly out of the constriction of the birth canal was less risky than a head being forced out quickly into sudden expansion.

'Here he comes,' Sophie muttered and she achingly raised herself from her own squat to lift the baby slowly, holding shoulders and cheeks between her hands as the baby made an arc in front of his mother's belly. His head was born with chin, mouth and nose, then eyes and finally the whole baby was out.

Pearl sagged back onto her heels and then onto her back and Sophie wiped the still flaccid baby over with the shawl until his little limbs contracted in reflex and, after a few torturously long seconds, he took his first breath.

She pulled Pearl's T-shirt up and placed her son directly skin to skin across her chest.

At the first touch of his mother's skin he gasped and cried, which by this point was exactly what Sophie felt like doing herself. But there was no time for that.

Still checking baby breathed, Sophie waited until the umbilical cord stopped pulsating. If mum was anemic then baby could be too, and the placenta offered a free blood transfusion if she held off tying the cord. Once that happened, Grandmother tied the twine where Sophie indicated, and baby was totally separated from his mother by the lethal looking knife they used to cut the cord.

Finally she could back away a little as the aunties crowded in.

Her hands shook and she wiped the sweat from her face with her forearm. More cord and placenta followed and a gush of bright blood seeped and began to form a pool under the new mum. 'Pearl.' Sophie leant in to catch the young woman's eye. 'I need to rub your tummy.'

Sophie nudged the grandmother and showed her how rubbing the now grapefruit sized uterus in Pearl's belly stopped the flow of blood until the uterus was a hard nub beneath their fingers.

The grandmother nodded and brought her gnarled hand in over Sophie's. Sophie wondered if one day another woman would be lucky that the grandmother remembered.

Another aunty knelt and gathered baby, then put Pearl's newborn to her mother's breast. The women knew this bit.

Sophie sat back and drew a deep breath. Baby whimpered and then cried again before he latched and began to suck. They didn't need her anymore and she had to get out of here before she fainted from the heat.

Chapter 9

It seemed hours since Sophie had disappeared inside the humpy.

Levi paced himself a worn strip under the tree as he watched the opening. He'd tried hand signals with the children as he attempted to take a health stock of those he could see, but it hadn't made the time pass faster.

Eventually he'd found an elder who conversed more easily, because Sophie would want to know. And there was only so much washing and drinking in the creek he could do when all the time he slaked his own thirst he knew she'd be parched. At least he'd soaked a cloth and filled her bottles for when she came out.

But he should have told her earlier about his qualifications, or at least discussed where he could help. The longer she'd spent inside with the women the deeper his guilt. An uncomfortable feeling he could have done without.

Not that he had a lot of experience with obstetrics, except for Odette's pregnancy and one small obstetric rotation that had him back peddling away from something with too much emotion attached, but he hadn't forgotten how helpful it could be to have another medical person to discuss things with.

His own career path had opted for something he could achieve on his own, something technical he could master and something he'd decided on when his brother went blind - and he'd been very successful.

Though the last two years had been hard. He'd driven himself to work outrageous hours and almost burnt out, he realized now, which was why Odette and his colleagues had been keen for him to have a break.

It was also why it felt so different to smile around Sophie so often.

Then again perhaps a near-death helicopter crash could make you appreciate the positives in life, too.

But that didn't help his guilt about Sophie.

Apart from his sister, he'd been accountable to no one since his brother died. Busy enough concentrating on his work and ensuring Odette was happy.

As for women, he had female medical acquaintances, occasional women friends with benefits that suited them both with the lack of strings, but none had left him with doubts about his behavior like this outback wonder woman did.

But life had changed when the unexpected happened. He'd disliked his father but that didn't mean he'd sit by if he'd met his death by foul means. And now Odette's and his own life had been put at risk. Let alone William and Sophie being collateral damage. The thought left him coldly furious. Someone was willing to risk everything to wipe them out.

When Sophie finally unbent herself from the humpy Levi felt the air whoosh out of his lungs as his shoulders dropped with relief. He saw the way she drew a deep breath and gathered herself. He remembered she did that a lot and it said volumes for her stamina and inner strength.

Another thing to add to the host of traits he admired about her.

He'd bet the air outside seemed cooler, especially as it approached sunset. The sound of a very new baby roaring his lungs out followed her and his heart eased more at the good result. This woman continued to amaze him.

For the briefest moment he thought he recognised something in her eyes when she looked at him that made the stress of waiting worthwhile... and brought back the guilt ten-fold.

Sophie almost cried at the sight of Levi and the release of stress made her want to throw herself into his arms for comfort. But she needed to wash and drink lots of fluids, and she needed not to think about all the things that could have gone wrong that hadn't.

Levi took her arm gently and sat her down under the welcome shade of a tree. 'Sit.' He handed her a water bottle and she took a long drink with her eyes closed. It felt so good to be away from the expectant eyes of the family. Even though she acknowledged how brave the grandmother had been to let Sophie lead the birth.

'Another amazing job?'

She opened her eyes, glanced around at the plains surrounding them, and sighed. 'Footling breech. We were all lucky.'

Exhaustion hit her and she sagged back against the knobby trunk behind her.

Levi gave her a searching look. 'I'll get you another drink.' He handed her some damp cloths. 'Here's something to wash with until you're up to a walk to the creek.'

He'd torn both sleeves off his shirt and soaked them. Brilliant. Amazing. Just what she needed.

When he offered them to her she could have hugged him, or for a brief mad second, run her hands over the bulge of his upper arms that were very nicely displayed by his newly sleeveless shirt.

Instead she wiped her hands with one, and once her fingers were reasonably clean, her face with the other. The cool dampness felt like it sizzled against her hot cheeks and brows. The coolness against her forehead was worth a hundred of the facials her ex had insisted she have.

When she opened her eyes she soaked in the sight of the man in front of her. There was something about a guy in a shirt without sleeves that called to her – not that she'd noticed this strange fetish before – no doubt because that man supplied what she wanted most.

Her appreciation must have shown in her face because he gave her a lopsided grin. 'I've been to the shop. Maybe you'd like a Kakadu Plum?'

The giggle surprised her. Probably hysteria but the release of emotion actually felt good. A little out of control, but healthy.

He was cosseting her again and she wallowed in it for a few indulgent seconds while she wiped her hands again with a clean corner of the damp material. A safe harbor to come out to. Strong arms when she needed them.

In fact, she could appreciate this man more and more, though she wouldn't fall for him. He made her feel crazily alive and special. Not going there! But she was glad he was here with her.

'There's hope for you yet.' She looked across at him but he only grimaced and her euphoria dimmed. He didn't look as happy as she felt.

Levi looked away and rubbed his neck, and to Sophie, the afternoon suddenly seemed stifling again. 'I'm glad,' he said, 'because there's something else I have to tell you.'

Lightly spoken but determined and her stomach sank as she wondered how much bad news a person could take in one day. And by the look on his face, she knew this was bad.

'The good news.' She was too weary for the bad at this minute. 'Please.'

'From what I gather, our tracker was on his way back when he found us and the Flying Doctor is coming for your girl. We'll be able to use their radio when they land.'

Her shoulders dropped in a heartfelt sigh. Not just good. 'That's great news.'

The day would work out. This whole draining adventure would end. She could get home in the not too distant future, shower and have a cup of tea and maybe she and Levi - and the others of course, she hastened to remind herself - could share that steak she'd kill for.

She didn't want to hear the bad news. Not now. She glanced around for something to divert him.

Barefoot, dark-eyed children huddled into a little giggling group to one side and darted mischievous glances across to where Sophie and Levi sat. 'Have you been making friends while I've been busy?'

He smiled at the children and pulled a silly face, which sent them off into a new fit of giggles. 'My new besties.'

So, he was good with kids too. She felt the warmth expand in her stomach. He really did have qualities she admired but it was far too early to think about the future.

Concentrate on now, Sophie. On this moment.

She looked from him to the little brown bodies that had begun to poke and wriggle amongst themselves. These children looked lean, but full of energy. 'I wonder if the kids are up to date with their immunizations?'

'Apparently,' he said a little smugly and she had to smile. 'I asked an elder. And they look well.'

He'd asked? Why? Because she'd said once she wanted to know? More warm and fuzzies buzzed in her belly and she smiled up at him. 'You've been busy. Anyone I need to look at?'

He hesitated. 'There's another elder here almost blind with cataracts. He'd benefit from surgery.'

Sophie looked around the camp. Lean-tos, red dust, a couple of shady trees and the creek. 'It's hard to encourage elders to leave their home for something they've learnt to live with.'

Levi shook his head. 'He's sightless. The results would be brilliant.'

Sophie nodded. 'I know. But he has to have the money to travel to the doctor.'

'What money?' Levi looked at her. 'The operation is free in public hospitals.'

Sophie shrugged, only giving half her concentration as she began to relax. She watched the children. Sipped more water. Exhaled. The baby was fine. She'd done the right thing. And now the Flying Doctor could take over the care. She could unwind.

'He'd have to leave here, travel, live away from his family. And for these people the thought of an operation is beyond frightening.'

'It's a minor operation.' Levi was like a terrier and his intensity began to intrude on her equilibrium.

Something in the way he persisted made her look away from the children and back to him. She spoke slowly as the implications sparked a question, and then a creeping disquiet, that maybe she'd missed something?

Because she'd been blind? More blind than an elder with cataracts? And stupid? 'Do you have much experience at diagnosing cataracts?'

His eyes searched hers and she knew. Felt the red dusty world fall away from under her feet. Felt the heat in her cheeks as she flushed with embarrassment and not a little anger.

'I could have,' he said.

Her eyes narrowed as she looked into his face. The same wary expression as the first time she'd met him. The face of a liar.

All the boxes slid into place in her mind. The comments, the looks between his sister and himself, his "first aid", She tried to keep the hurt out of her voice. 'What sort of business did you say you had?'

'I didn't.' Still he looked at her so she had to break eye contact.

'And…?' she said to the children across the camp.

He paused, waited until she met his eyes again. 'I'm an ophthalmologist specializing in microsurgery. I have a very successful practice in Sydney.'

'You're a doctor?' Quietly. 'You said first aid.' Her voice dropped even lower. 'You lied again.'

His voice was low too. 'I didn't lie.'

'You didn't deny.' It hurt, actually it crushed her that she'd been fooled again. 'Liar by omission.'

'That was the bad news.'

What did he want, a pat on the head? It was bad alright. She'd started to like him. Like him a lot. Please don't think about anything else. She'd certainly begun to lean on him more than a little.

And he was a doctor. A rich doctor. And a liar.

Just like Brad. The man who'd stripped her heart and taken a part of her that had been precious and new and untarnished and stamped on it.

The way she'd ordered Levi around because she'd been the only medical person made her cringe. Did he understand how hard it had been to wear that responsibility? And now he tells her he's better qualified. Even if he was a specialist surgeon, he'd started as a generalist.

He could have put Smiley's shoulder in.

The weight of unshed tears made her face feel heavy. Like a big rock tied to her cheek pulling her whole face down. She blinked her stupid stinging eyes and gritted her teeth. No way was she wasting water on this creep.

'I'm struggling to think of a reason you wouldn't make this all easier on me. Was this some kind of test to see how much I'd take before I broke?'

He shook his head and his hand reached out. She wasn't touching him. They may as well be covered in slime.

He must have seen it because his hand dropped. 'Look. Sophie. I think you're amazing.' He dragged his hand through his hair. 'You didn't need my help.'

Holy cow. How dare he? She so didn't want to do this now. Or ever.

She climbed wearily to her feet and with her eyes fixed past his shoulder, she took off down the hill to the creek to gather herself, almost tripping in her haste to get away from him.

The water splashed cold against her fingers and she plunged her hands and forearms in to shock herself out of the stifling blanket of cottonwool she felt smothered in.

She'd been so close, had almost been attracted to exactly the type of man who could crush her, again, and in just a few short days.

Didn't she learn from her mistakes?

She washed her face, washed the salty trickles that weren't creek water, and then washed her face again.

Damn him. Damn him. Damn him.

Slowly composure returned, or at least her hands stopped shaking and her tears dried. Her head ached with a dense weariness that seemed to wrap around her bones and she forced tired feet to carry her back to the camp, but she walked straight past him to the humpy to check the mother and baby.

By the time she emerged she had control again and an impenetrable barrier around her. A barrier even higher than one of the domes of the Bungle Bungles.

The sound of an airplane droned in the distance and Sophie searched for the sight of it over the hills like she needed it to breathe. Her gaze sought anything in the sky instead of looking at Levi.

The sooner that plane landed the better. And the joke? She wasn't even worried about flying out of here.

She had to think of Odette, still out in the scrub, unaware that help was coming and the possibility of her labor. Once she was safe Sophie could release all responsibility. And she would.

When they made town he could worry about the disaster of the helicopter and she and Smiley could go home to their house. With just a little luck she'd never see the Sydney siblings again and she could forget what a fool she'd almost been.

After what seemed like hours the noise of the plane dominated the sky and the shadow crossed the ground in front of them as the pilot circled to land on the area the men had cleared.

'Bring it on,' Sophie said under her breath.

When the twin-engine aircraft landed, surprisingly smoothly on the rocky soil, the door opened, the ladder descended and three people climbed out. The doctor, Jock McDonald, was a Scottish larrikin who raised his eyebrows at the sight of Levi and Sophie. The nurse, who Sophie didn't recognize, strode purposefully towards them. The pilot waved but stayed to walk around the plane.

'There'll be a story here, I'm noo doubting,' Jock said to Sophie, whom he'd met at the clinic. He waved at Levi. 'I'll talk to you in a wee moment.'

The nurse hailed Sophie and the two women accompanied Jock into the humpy, suddenly critically crowded until the doctor shooed away all except the grandmother. He checked Pearl and scolded her in such a broad accent there wasn't a hope she'd understand anything he said.

But he smiled and patted her head when he'd finished, and again when he'd checked the tiny but vigorous baby over with obvious admiration.

'You're verra lucky. You'll both still come to the hospital so we can keep an eye on you for a day or two,' he said to Pearl and again to the grandmother. 'In case baby goes off his food. He's only a wee thing.'

Then he left the humpy and raised his eyebrows at Sophie. 'I'd like to hear your side of it. You did well, lassie.'

Sophie didn't feel anything but tired. 'Uncomplicated footling breech.'

'There's no such thing.'

Sophie smiled wanly. 'Everything went right. Hands off the breech until the head. Baby fine by a minute after birth. We weren't unlucky but we would have been up the creek if it hadn't panned out as well as it had.'

'Aye, but you weren't. So no use worryin' about the ones that go good like they're supposed to.'

He pulled his hand antiseptic from his pocket and offered it to Sophie and she lathered herself until even her nail beds gleamed. Unimaginable luxury.

Dr Jock inclined his head towards the tree. 'So, who's this big fella, and how're you two here?'

She shook her head. She didn't want to talk about it. 'He'll fill you in. Have you room for us?'

He looked at the plane. 'Och no, not for two, but we can contact the Bungles and they'll fly in and get him. We'll have to take the mother and child or she'll have no care if either get sick.' He gave her a searching look. 'I'm thinkin' you need to come with us.'

Then he crossed to where Levi was talking to the pilot beneath the tree, a map spread between them. The rescue mission would soon be underway. They had no need for her.

Fifteen minutes later, Sophie joined Pearl and her baby in the RFDS plane with Dr Jock while the nurse rode up front with the pilot.

Levi had been in contact with a helicopter service at the Bungles who were en route to pick him up. Another had flown to the crash site. More red tape would follow at a later date, but very shortly Odette and Smiley would be on their way back to the hospital at Kununurra.

Sophie could drop the last of her responsibilities.

An hour later she stepped out of the plane at the airport in Kununurra, too. But it wasn't where she wanted to be. She ached to go home, back to her own space, a place to hide and lick her wounds and take stock of the new disaster she'd brought on herself, but she'd have to wait for the hospital to release her brother.

The nurse from the flight lent her flat keys and spare clothes, and Sophie spent an hour soaking red dust from her legs and her hair in a long bath that should have relaxed her but didn't.

She could hear the sound of helicopters taking off and landing at the airfield across the road and the sound grated across her ears like gravel over her skin.

No doubt one of them held "him". All the time she berated herself. She should have never let her guard down, couldn't believe she'd done it again, been tricked by the words and caresses of a smooth-talking liar. But never again.

Levi watched the entrance to the hospital as cars with lights drove up and deposited people. Watched every taxi, truck, and bus that pulled up. He watched families walking and couples talking and single women who didn't matter, but nowhere did he see a pony-tail in an Akubra hat that quickened his heart.

It was night now but this day never seemed to end.

He'd spent an hour at the police station. The aircraft crash investigation team were coming from Perth and until then nothing could be proved, but they were on alert.

He wasn't having his sister put at risk again. Or Sophie. Never again.

He'd arranged a light aircraft to fly them all home. For him and Odette, the men at Xanadu had put the landing lights out on the strip. At Jabiru Township he'd arranged another set for Sophie and William.

Nobody, especially him, had spotted Sophie, but Smiley had heard from her on the phone.

She'd been on the ground for two hours now, he'd checked, she should be here soon.

He still didn't know what to say.

She hadn't allowed him a word since he'd confessed, hadn't looked at him before she left, but the hurt in her eyes had bitten harder than he'd expected. He just hoped she'd cool down and then he could explain before he had to take Odette back to Sydney.

The digital clock in the hospital foyer flashed ten past nine and a taxi pulled up. There she was. Strangely smaller than he remembered, in a pair of long trousers that didn't suit her as much as her shorts. The toss of her head when she saw him gave a pretty accurate picture of what she thought. Not a good omen for explanations.

Fair enough. Maybe he deserved it. No "maybe" about it.

There was too much happening now, but later he'd try to explain. It seemed his sister had come through the ordeal unscathed. He wasn't so sure that Sophie had, and it was all his fault.

She lifted her hat off and held it in her hand as if to ward him off. The way she walked past him with her head down made him want to kick himself. He fell in behind her as she headed for the casualty until he caught up. 'You okay?'

Sophie gritted her teeth. 'I'm fine!' Was this guy for real? She didn't look at him.

'Sophie. Let me explain.'

'I'd prefer you didn't.' She stopped. 'Look, Levi. Dr whatever-your-name-is.' That was when she realized how deep the perfidy went. 'I don't even know your last name.'

'Pearson.'

The name rang a bell. Pearson? Pearson? But she couldn't place it. She shrugged it off with a tiny shake of her head. Was it really Pearson? Who could tell with this guy?

Levi stared down at her. 'Don't you think you're being a little harsh, considering what we've been through together?'

'I really don't care if you think I'm harsh. I'm tired. I'm over this. I have to see you for the next hour but I don't have to listen. I'd appreciate it if you'd respect that.'

They sat in opposite ends of the small waiting room in silence.

To start with Sophie flicked through a magazine but on every page of upmarket advertising, she could imagine Levi driving that car. Eating at that restaurant. Dancing with that girl. Wearing that suit.

She threw the magazine down and leaned back in the chair and closed her eyes. She hadn't lost her heart to another city slicker. She hadn't.

Finally, after another torturous half hour the patients were released. Odette hugged her and Smiley nodded and even put his hand on Sophie's shoulder and squeezed it.

'Thanks, Sis.'

'We were lucky,' she mumbled, and reached up and gave him a kiss. She needed to dwell on the fact that all of them were alive and that it had been pretty close. Maybe that was why she felt weepy.

Sophie avoided Levi's attempt to catch her eye and she only then wondered how they were getting home. Not by helicopter she hoped.

'I've hired a plane to get us back,' he said as if she'd asked the question out loud.

She risked a glance and found him looking at her. 'Thank you,' she mumbled but that was all.

Smiley would fly on to Xanadu, stay the night to collect his vehicle and drive home tomorrow. Sophie would be dropped home to sleep. First stop Jabiru Town. Yes, please. Sophie couldn't wait.

The flight was short and when she finally closed her front door behind her, she leaned against it with a heartrending sigh. The wood was hard and scratchy from peeling paint and she rubbed her head against it as if to rub some sense into her brain.

What had she done?

Sleep proved impossible after the events of the last two days and, ridiculously, the most disturbing factor was Levi's decision to keep her unaware of his profession.

Somewhere inside a voice said it was trivial, not worth crying over, but still the tears trickled. She needed to get back to work and forget her adventures, her weakness, and the high-flying people at Xanadu.

Chapter 10

When Sophie opened the front door two days later she glanced across the street and saw Levi leaning on the veranda rail of the clinic as if he owned it.

There he was. Designer jeans and expensive watch flashing in the sunlight, and there she was, clutching her throat like a wimp. She would have pulled back, hidden inside, if he hadn't straightened when he saw her, but it was too late. Too darn late.

Her hand needed prying off the handle as she pulled the door shut behind her, and when she crossed the veranda it felt like a creek full of crocodiles were shifting under foot. What could he possibly want? She hated that it mattered so much it made her ache.

The dusty road, usually wide in the sunlight, seemed narrow today and in far too little time she stood beside him. Just a drift of some expensive aftershave letting her know he was still from another world. 'How can I help you, Doctor?'

His eyes narrowed and when he spoke his voice was very low. 'Don't call me Doctor and don't talk to me as if you don't know me.'

She blinked. Was he trying for best defense is attack? Well, she could do a little attacking of her own.

'I thought you'd be long gone.'

He sighed. 'I can see the thought of that upsets you no end.'

'Hmmm.' The deserted street didn't produce any distractions so she had to look at him. 'Perhaps not.' She shrugged. 'Self-preservation's like that. Nothing personal. How can I help you?'

'I have to stay in the area for the crash investigation team. It looks as if the chopper was definitely tampered with and there's a police investigation. I thought you should know.'

Ice trickled down her neck despite the heat. What? Deliberate sabotage? With a pregnant Odette on board?

'Tampered with? That's horrible. Who'd want to do that?' She had no idea, but it seemed the concept wasn't new to him. How surprising he hadn't shared that with her earlier.

'There's some suspicion on Steve, the resort manager. He's disappeared.'

'Steve?' She shook her head at the crazy notion. 'I don't understand.'

He ran his hand through his hair. 'It's a long story.'

Long stories take time. That meant he'd stay longer and she didn't think she could take that. 'No problem.' She couldn't help the tiny bitterness that laced her words. She forced herself to hold out her hand and braced for that frisson she felt every time she touched him. 'All the best then.'

He looked down at her fingers but made no move to take her hand. 'I was hoping we could part as friends.'

She shrugged, not without a little relief, and tucked her hand away safely by her side. She didn't want to be his special friend. They came from different worlds. Had different morals. 'I don't think so.' Blowed if she'd hold her hand out again. 'When are you allowed to leave?'

'It's taken a day to get the team in from Perth. The preliminary reports will be through late this afternoon and we leave tomorrow. I tried to send Odette back today but she refused to go without me.'

She could understand that. Especially when she'd just found out someone tried to kill her. The idea was almost too far-fetched to believe. 'She's been through a lot. I guess it would make anyone nervous to travel on their own, let alone late in pregnancy.'

Unconsciously she wiped both palms down her shorts. Already she could feel the moisture on her skin, and still he hadn't come to the reason for his presence.

He paused, as if waiting for her response, and when she remained silent he went on, as if he wasn't comfortable either. Good, she thought.

'At least Odette didn't have her baby in the Bungles. My biggest fear. I should have made her stay in Sydney.'

To be fair – not that she really felt like being fair – Sophie didn't see that. Odette was her own woman and well past the age of consent. But it was none of her business. Right?

She couldn't take much more of this. 'Why are you here?'

He stepped forward and she stepped back until her back was against the unopened door. Very gently his fingertip lifted her chin until he could see into her eyes.

His touch was cool and firm against the heat in her skin, and his gaze captured hers as easily as – was it only a week ago? – she'd first seen him. Despite the sensible need to do so, she couldn't look away. When she didn't push his finger away the other fingers came until his hand rested on her cheek, cupping her chin, and they stared at each other.

Now, after the time they'd spent together, she knew his grey irises held rings of blue, his lashes were dark brown not black, and memories of that time she'd felt his skin against her cheek and his mouth against hers made her shoulders droop with comfort as if he'd done it again.

Why did he have to touch her?

Those times in Levi's arms were a whole different world – one she wasn't going to get used to – and unfortunately those few touches had been indelible. How much more proof did she need to get out of this situation? Imagine if he could read now how much she grieved his loss.

'I'm sorry you've been involved in this, Sophie. I'd like the chance to sit and talk before I go.'

Step sideways, move away – the litany in her head drowned out his words. But her body didn't obey. So she tried to concentrate on what he said to block out his eyes on hers and the feel of his hand.

Finally, her body responded and she pulled her chin away and walked back to the rail with her back to him. She couldn't sit and talk! No way. 'Was there something you wanted to ask about your sister's pregnancy?'

He came to stand beside her, his shoulder close to hers but not touching. 'It's nothing to do with Odette,' he said with a skyward glance of frustration. 'It's about the way we parted after extreme circumstances. I don't like that I've upset you.'

Upset? Not the word she'd have chosen. He'd hurt her badly and she didn't know why it mattered so much. She'd have to let him talk; she didn't have to listen. There'd be no other way to get rid of him.

She held up her hands. 'I don't want to talk about it, but talk if you have to. I'm over it.'

He searched her face. 'I'm not over it... over your distress.' His scrutiny seemed almost abrasive to her skin but she blocked it out.

'What happened to you in the past is not me. Can't you forgive me for not being more open with you?'

Nope. She was too darn scared it was the tip of the iceberg of deceit she hadn't discovered yet. Too terrified if she trusted again she would break a part of her that would never heal.

She shook her head and looked back in time to a hurt that was nothing to this.

'I can't help how the past has shaped me. Men who can't tell the truth seem drawn to me. We have a family history of being scammed by liars.' She risked a glance at his face. 'I'm a simple girl, Levi. I say what I mean. Right now my meaning is simple. I want you to go.'

He rubbed the back of his neck. 'What do you want me to say, Sophie? I'm sorry I misled you but there are things going on here you don't know about.' He waved at the distant hills. 'If I told you then you could be in danger.'

She shook her head. Not good enough. 'There's nothing more to say then.'

He frowned at her. 'You're not giving me a chance.'

'Tough.' She shrugged her shoulders at him but they felt as heavy as if she carried a yoke with two loaded buckets. When he raised his brows at her, like she was the one being childish, she actually felt like that child. A small disgruntled one, who'd discovered the world isn't magical anymore.

He'd held back the truth just when she'd started to believe she might have found a man she could trust her heart to. A man who warmed her when he looked at her and listened when she was off on her tangent. One who stretched her mind and made her laugh and had a strong hand she could hold when she needed... and arms that comforted.

She'd thought she'd seen things in Levi that she hadn't seen in any man before. But now she doubted herself, and him, again. She didn't have any reserves left. 'Please, just go.'

His face shut down until he looked like the stranger she'd seen on the first day. Aloof, arrogant, then finally dismissive. 'I'm sorry you feel that way.' He turned but before he left he asked, 'Where's William?'

Confusion held her answer. William? Smiley. 'Work. He's mustering cattle. Why?' Would he never go? Her eyes stung and her throat bulged so thick with tears she could barely breathe.

'Something's come out about the family that used to own Xanadu. Do you know what their name was?'

She didn't have the energy to talk about her foolish, gullible grandfather. It was easier to say, 'No. Why?'

'Nothing important.' He took a step towards her and she panicked that she'd throw herself into his arms. She stepped back as if he'd raised his hand and her panic must have shown on her face. That stopped him. And made him wince.

'Goodbye, Sophie.'

He stepped off the veranda into the dust, and as he walked away, she realized she'd done what she'd blamed him for. She'd lied to him. And not just about her grandfather.

Levi drove back to Xanadu too fast, which involved concentration on the road, but he was grimly thankful for that. He didn't want to think. Didn't want to relive the distress he'd recognised in Sophie's eyes. The disgust.

It was probably safer she wasn't seen with him anyway. Safer for her because he could feel the danger closing in. If the results came back as he expected then it upped the ante for Steve.

They were all in danger.

Two hours later Smiley burst into the clinic as Sophie sutured a nasty gash from a poorly wielded chainsaw.

The young jackaroo had been lucky he'd only touched his leg on the way through the log and had opened the skin in one thick stripe. Sophie looked up. People burst in often, but never Smiley.

She took one look at his face. 'Odette?'

'She rang me on the satellite phone. Her waters broke, and the contractions are coming every three minutes. She's refusing to move and they're at the Pentecost crossing. Then the phone died.'

That didn't make sense. 'The same spot I saw Levi the first day? Why would they go there?'

Smiley shook his head at the delay. 'It's where her father was taken.'

Her father? Taken? It all came back. Crocodiles. "Pearson". When Levi told her his surname at Kununurra, she knew it rung a bell. She couldn't believe she'd forgotten. Such was the state Levi had her in.

The name of the people her grandfather had lost the family station to. Levi hadn't been a guest, he'd been the freakin' owner.

No wonder they could use the choppers, drive the vehicles, do whatever they wished.

And that question about her family?

More subterfuge if not an outright lie.

She yanked the final suture through and the unfortunate young cowboy yelped in protest. Sophie bit her lip and looked at the jackaroo. 'Oops, sorry.'

She tied off, snipped the ends of the suture and put a see-through dressing over the top in minimal time. 'Keep it dry. Come back in a week and I'll take the stitches out.'

The young bloke glanced at her once as if to say, 'I'll take 'em out myself,' then scurried out of the room. Sophie sighed. She'd never have done that before Levi had disrupted her life.

'Xanadu.' She looked at her brother. 'They own it.'

So many lies. Smiley didn't look surprised. Geez. More unpalatable truth. 'You knew?' Of course he did.

Impatiently. 'Odette asked me not to say anything because she wasn't even supposed to tell me.'

'For goodness sake, why not?' Now these people were infecting Smiley with their stupid intrigue.

Smiley shook his head. 'Odette's in labor. Come on. Get what you need. It's not important and I really don't care. Let's go.'

He was right.

Smiley, a man who never moved fast, drove as if driving the Dakar rally and they made the crossing in an hour. A Kimberley record that Sophie never wanted to break.

Her teeth still rattled in her head and the dust stung her eyes but she didn't say anything. Smiley's words repeated in her head. 'It's not important. I really don't care.' Kept in the dark by Levi? Why did it matter in the big scheme of things? She didn't want to think what she could have risked if Levi had a good reason to hold back information.

Smiley was right. Now wasn't the time. It didn't matter. She needed to put any emotion over Levi's reticence aside and think about Odette.

She squeezed the emergency delivery pack on her lap and ran over a few scenarios. At least when she'd felt Odette's uterus the baby had palpated as cephalic; head first was better than breech. Plus, she had medical back up in Levi, she thought bitterly.

Why wouldn't Levi just pick his sister up and move her? Surely he didn't agree with her having a baby out in the wilderness. She'd never understand these people.

When they arrived she saw why they were still there.

Levi's vehicle sat low to the ground with four flat tires, a very reasonable excuse for staying put.

The local police vehicle had pulled up next to them and one of the officers was talking on the two-way radio.

Smiley pulled up in a shower of gravel and threw himself out of the car towards Odette, who sat with her back against a Boab in her trousers and bra. Where was her shirt? Then she burst into tears when she saw him. Sophie blinked. That was different.

Levi sat next to her with his arm around her until Smiley took his place.

Sophie glanced back at the river, which wasn't far enough away from them, and scanned the bank. Two large saltwater crocodiles sat patiently at the opposite edge and watched them with unblinking yellow eyes. Yikes.

She frowned over the half-dressed Odette lost in Smiley's arms. Any reserve against Levi forgotten she turned to him. 'You okay?'

'Will be,' he said grimly. 'Satellite phone went flat after we got through to the police and William.'

She frowned. He didn't look right. 'Are you hurt?'

'Stray bullet nicked me. It's nothing.' He lifted his arm from his side where he'd had it tucked and showed a wad of heavily bloodstained material tied around his left arm. She guessed it was Odette's shirt.

Her pulse rate jumped as if *she'd* been shot. 'Let me see.'

'Check on Odette first.' He stepped back, still giving orders, but she suspected she wouldn't get to see until she'd checked his sister.

Sophie scanned his Odette quickly but carefully. 'You okay, Odette?'

Odette spoke from Smiley's arms. 'I am now.' She didn't sound like a woman in the final throes of labor.

She turned back to Levi. 'Right, now show me.'

'It happened before the police came. When we first got out of the car.' He glared at her and held up his arm. 'We don't have time for this. If he's still around he could shoot again.'

Sophie busied herself undoing the material. 'I'm assuming we're on the right side of the tree for safety, yes?'

Levi nodded a brief response. 'Unless he moved.'

She inclined her head toward the river. 'The police will protect us from the shooter but not from that couple of saltwater crocodiles who fancy a piece of you, too.'

He raised his brows at her. 'It must be your fate in life to warn me about crocodiles.'

'And yours to keep me in the dark when everyone else has all the information. But we'll talk about that later.'

Gingerly he held his injured arm as she eased the wad away from the skin below his shoulder to expose a neat "in" hole and a less neat "out" hole through torn flesh. The bullet had passed through in a jagged tunnel without causing major damage, but blood oozed sluggishly as soon as she took the pressure away. She hastily put the wad back.

He was right. It wouldn't kill him.

Levi's indrawn breath made her wince. 'Sorry.'

'It's nothing. I'll heal. We have to get Odette away from here.'

The man was mad. 'I imagine the police will get us all away from here.'

Short, sharp shake of his head. 'I'm not going anywhere until I find him,' he growled.

Her incredulous impatience rose.

She gestured to his shoulder. 'Not like that surely?'

'Someone shot at us while Odette was saying goodbye. Here. Shot the tires on the car. Tried to kill my sister. He's still out there, I know it, even though the police think he's gone.'

His eyes burned into hers and she shivered a little with his implacable determination to go after the shooter.

His voice inflexible, he said, 'I'm staying until we get him. Now, please do what I ask and take Odette. If you stay here he'll try to kill you too.'

She glanced at Smiley who was attempting to disentangle Odette and calm her at the same time. He looked up at Sophie. 'Let's get 'em out of here.'

The bullet hit the tree beside them a millisecond before the shot rang out.

Smiley scooped Odette like she was a feather and dived around the back of the tree. Levi grabbed Sophie and wrapped her in his arms and down onto the ground where he rolled them both her behind the tree. He flattened himself on top of her. The breath whooshed from her lungs as a bunch of dead boab leaves crackled under her back. She hoped there were no snakes sleeping under there.

The gunman had moved. Obviously. And she'd been shot at.

She didn't want to get shot. But she didn't want Levi to protect her with his body, either. Did he want to get shot again?

She sucked in another labored breath.

He was darned heavy but she doubted he'd listen to her right at this moment.

Thankfully, when no further shots rang out, he eased himself off and let her go but he kept his body between her and the direction the bullet had come from.

'You okay?' he asked.

She nodded. The fact that he'd cared enough to protect her made her eyes sting. Though maybe he'd have done it for any woman. She shouldn't read anything into his strong chest squeezing against hers while she'd been in his arms.

As they crouched and awkwardly dusted themselves off, Sophie could see a fresh splash of blood in the dirt beside her. Levi had dislodged the makeshift bandage and his wound oozed lazily again. 'Come here,' she said and resettled the wadding as she frowned at him. Her fingers busied themselves until she had it adjusted to her satisfaction.

His hand caught hers. 'Thank you.'

'Any time.' She couldn't help the heat that rode in her cheeks.

He raised his brows. 'I might take you up on that.'

'This guy means business,' Smiley commented grimly, breaking into the moment, with the four of them crouched behind the thankfully wide trunk of the fat boab. The police had dived behind their own car and one of them fired back.

Levi grimaced. 'I'm so sorry you two are involved in this.'

She looked from one man to the other. 'Involved in what? Is there a plan? Now, what is it I don't know about?' Sophie demanded.

Levi sighed. 'You know the helicopter was definitely sabotaged.'

She nodded. Smiley had shared that. Not Levi.

'I'm now convinced my father was pushed into the river here five months ago. Whoever did that is shooting at us now.'

He paused. Let out a breath as if he didn't want to say the words. 'I think it's my newly discovered half-brother. Steve. The manager at Xanadu.'

She did not believe this. 'Steve's your half-brother?' This was outback Australia, not some gangland setting. Who were these people?

Levi must have seen her confusion. 'Because of Xanadu. It seems that my step-sibling expected to inherit the property, and he wants it. Will do anything to get it.'

He pulled her in close with his good arm. His eyes suddenly intent and she stilled. Her heart rate picked up. 'In case we all die here, there's something you need to hear. I think you are the most amazing woman I've ever met.' Then his mouth came down onto hers and he kissed her. Properly. Delightfully. Crazy man.

He'd kissed her. In the middle of a gunfight. And by the look on his face he'd enjoyed it. Yep. He was mad. 'You must be delirious. We're being SHOT AT!'

'That's why it seemed a good idea to tell you now.' He stroked her cheek. 'And I'm not lying.'

The sound of a vehicle revving and then driving away had Smiley peering around the tree. 'Could have been someone else parked and they got scared,' Smiley said.

Levi hit the tree with the flat of his hand and then winced as the vibration ran through his body to his injured shoulder. 'Or could be our man.'

The police car started up and the officers sped off in pursuit. 'It seems the coppers agree,' Smiley said.

'Damn. Wish I'd seen the car,' Levi growled, 'Priorities. Let's get the girls out of here and back to Xanadu.'

Smiley nodded grimly and went for the truck to reverse it back to Odette. Sophie slid down the tree next to Odette to see how she fared. 'You okay, honey?'

Head down, Odette held her stomach. She whimpered. 'I think the baby's coming.' Then a tiny strangled moan had Sophie peer at her with a frown.

'We might just sit for a minute,' Sophie said to no one in particular, and rested her hand on Odette's arm. Softly she asked, 'What's happening?'

Odette turned agonized eyes to Sophie and whispered. 'I need to go to the bathroom.'

Sophie looked at Levi, who had frozen at his sister's words. 'I think she's pushing.'

Chapter 11

'No. Not here.' Levi cast his eyes skywards, but all he could see were the sparse leaves of the boab above him. He could handle the idea of being shot at but not the birth of Odette's baby.

He needed her safe, with doctors, and theatres, and sterile surroundings. He couldn't lose Odette like his mother. In childbirth. His worst nightmare.

He'd failed every aspect of keeping his sister safe. He'd involved her in a helicopter crash, a shooting, and now this. He wanted her out of here and all she needed to do was walk. Just walk to the car. Get in.

'Please stand up, Odette.'

'You can't prioritize this.' Sophie shook her head at him. 'She's pushing. It's coming. Now.'

Prioritize? What on earth was she talking about? He wanted his sister in a nice safe hospital, end of story.

'Come on Odette. You have to get up.'

Odette looked at him and he could see the fear behind her tremulous smile. 'Sorry. Love to. Can't do.'

He looked at Sophie and despite the sympathy he saw in her eyes she shook her head. She was right. Typical. Again.

The truck backed up to them and Smiley jumped out. 'Let's go.'

Levi looked helplessly down at both women, distanced from him by their silent communication. 'Sophie says Odette's having the baby.'

'She can't have it here.' Smiley cast a quick glance to the river. 'The crocs will have the lot of us if we don't get out of here.'

'Then make sure they don't,' Sophie said with a touch of asperity. 'She'll move as soon as the baby's born.'

'Tell the men to go away,' Odette whispered.

Sophie obliged. 'Go do your job. We're busy doing ours.'

Smiley blinked, nodded and drifted away to keep watch between them and the river.

Levi looked down at Sophie, who had come into their lives and continued to cope with one disaster after another. Thank God she was here.

What would they do without her? What would *he* do without her? He had no idea.

When had everything changed?

When had Sophie become more important than the guilt he lived? More important than finding his father's killer. More important to protect than himself?

Sophie and Odette leaned with their backs against the tree. 'You concentrate on listening to your body and I'll worry about everything else. Just breathe it out,' she said quietly and looked up at him. 'I need the kit out of the truck and the rugs I brought, please.'

At least it seemed he could be of some use.

He left and returned with what she'd asked. 'Where do you want these?'

'Spread around us, except for the thin rug – the yellow one. Put that over Odette. Then pass me the pack and the towel. Thanks.'

She helped Odette adjust her clothing beneath the yellow rug, then undid the delivery pack and laid the cord clamps aside. She drew up the Syntocinon for after the birth, washed her hands with antiseptic, then pulled on the gloves. Odette had shifted to a squat and had her back resting against the trunk for support.

'A little primitive but this tree has great facilities compared to the camp the other day.'

Levi strangled back an inappropriate laugh. He supposed it did and he watched her lean back against the tree next to his sister and wait. Her capable hands were clasped loosely on her lap. As if this were just another April day in the Kimberley.

How would he go back to Sydney? How could he leave her? Except for the minor fact she wouldn't have him.

Odette looked up once, an arrested expression on her face, as she stared at Sophie. 'William said you told him birthing a baby was like having a foal or a calf.'

Sophie brushed the hair off Odette's forehead with her finger and smiled. She had a great smile, Levi thought as he pretended not to listen.

'He's a bad boy for repeating that. I said that to reassure him with the familiar, because he was scared for you. But you're doing so well it might be true.'

He saw the tears fill his sister's eyes and Odette sniffed. 'I want to go home. I can't believe I'm doing this. Having my baby here.'

This was all his fault.

Sophie rolled her eyes and she glanced at him quickly before looking back at Odette. 'After meeting you two, with all the drama you bring... I can believe it.'

Odette's laugh was cut short by the next pain and Levi winced as it dragged a low groan from her as the baby moved down.

Levi twisted his hands. He felt so damn powerless. Couldn't do anything for either of them.

'Beautiful,' said Sophie, in that quiet, almost hypnotic voice he'd never be able to match. 'Slow breaths. Not long now.'

She looked up and frowned when she saw him watching her. He stretched his lips into a strained smile but she must have seen his tension.

'Take a few breaths, too, Levi. It's okay.'

He was always in trouble with this woman. 'Can I get you anything, Sophie?'

'Sip of water for Odette, thanks. There's a bottle in the truck. And maybe check on Smiley. I'll call if we need you.'

In other words, his marching orders. Okay. Maybe he would be better out of the way until it was all over.

'Call him William!' Odette mumbled through gritted teeth as she finished the pain and breathed out.

Levi handed her the water and drifted away. Sophie watched him go. He appeared resigned to the inevitable now, finally, that his sister was doing what he'd dreaded all along. Sophie couldn't guarantee everything would be fine, she could just assume it would, and deal with the variations as they came.

And Levi would be there for support if she needed him. She seemed to have found a well of faith in him and she didn't quite know where it had grown from. Maybe even a good person to have around. She could've become used to that.

Odette gripped her hand and Sophie refocused where she should have been all along.

Odette panted and bit her lip. 'I don't think I want to do this.'

Sophie closed her fingers around Odette's shoulder in support. 'I know. Let it happen. Just push your tummy out as you breathe in, and let it fall as you breathe out, and the baby will move down.'

Odette breathed and finally Sophie could see the first signs of descent. 'I can see some dark hair now, Odette, so he's not bald.'

Odette's eyes stared into hers as she searched Sophie's face. 'The contraction's gone and it's burning.'

'As it should,' Sophie said quietly. 'Everything needs to stretch and baby's head sitting there is the best way to do that.'

'I am so not doing this again,' Odette ground out as she panted the pain away. Then her voice changed. 'Can I touch him?'

Sophie smiled, she loved this bit, and took Odette's hand to guide it down to the baby's head. 'Of course.'

Odette stretched tentatively until she realized there was a hard little scalp right under her fingers and her hand jumped away. 'Oh my, Lord. This is so not right.'

'Afraid it is.' Sophie smiled. 'The next pain will move baby out more, just remember to push slowly with your breath. You don't want your baby to come out too fast.'

'I don't?' She whistled her breath in between her teeth. 'You've got to be kidding.'

Odette closed her eyes and breathed and by inches the baby descended. Sophie stroked Odette's hair out of her eyes. 'You are amazing, you know that?'

The next contraction built and the amount of baby's head grew slowly as Odette breathed him out.

Wrinkled forehead, eyes and nose, and finally mouth and chin until the whole head rotated to face his mother's leg. Sophie dried the little face and hair gently as they waited for the next contraction.

'He's blinking,' she told Odette.

Odette panted. 'But his body's not out.'

'He's awake, that's for sure.'

And as Odette pushed for the last time, baby eased into Sophie's hands and she ran the towel over him as he opened his eyes wider – a dark, dark blue – and he blinked as he looked around.

'It really is a boy? I have my son?' She eased down the tree to sit and stretched her legs out in front of her. Then, 'He's not crying,' as Sophie lifted him up his mother's body, warm damp skin to his mother's, until he lay across Odette's breasts. She covered them both with the rug and tucked the edges in.

'He doesn't have to, he's breathing. He's pink and happy to be on you. And yes, he's definitely a boy.'

Sophie gave the injection, clamped and cut the cord and waited for the third stage to complete. When it was over she checked Odette's uterus through her soft belly skin, and found it rock-like beneath her fingers. Everything had gone as it should. She pulled the rug back again and checked Odette's pulse.

'It's over.' Odette smiled up at her. 'I've done it.' Her smile seemed to light up ten feet around them. She glanced with wonder down at her son. 'You helped me do that.'

'My privilege.' They sat there quietly for a minute or two. Just breathing and allowing the peace of the bush to steal over them. To appreciate the wonder of childbirth in such a primitive setting. The baby squirmed and Odette laughed and stroked his head and she glanced at Sophie. Their eyes met and they both smiled.

'Can you ask Levi and William to come see him now, please?' The softness in those powerful new-mother's eyes made it hard for Sophie to swallow and her eyes stung. This was why she loved this job.

'Sure.' Sophie tucked a little escaping hand back under the blankets and stripped off her gloves. 'Congratulations. You were amazing.'

'Thank you, Sophie. I just let you worry about everything else.' She stroked the downy head as her son wrinkled his forehead and blinked up at her. 'He's so gorgeous.'

Sophie stroked his tiny hand that escaped again and nodded. She signaled Levi over and watched the men fuss over mother and baby. Her face ached with a broad goofy smile that faded with just a tinge of melancholy for what might have been.

She walked towards the river to keep watch.

A few minutes later Levi stood and crossed the grass to her side and she stepped back to a safer distance. He smiled ruefully, and then stepped forward and deliberately stepped in closer to invade her space. 'You are getting a hug whether you like it or not.'

'Oh.' She didn't know what to say to that and in the end she didn't have to say anything as Levi lifted his good arm and drew her against his chest. She sighed against him. She was glad he insisted. She knew it was true, she'd wanted this hug.

'Thank you, Sophie,' he said quietly, and they stood there with the sound of the river gurgling behind them and the raucous laugh of a kookaburra punctuating their isolation. His arm was warm and heavy around her shoulders and the amount of comfort she gained was disproportionate to the gesture. Felt so good.

She lent her head more heavily against the uninjured side of his body for a few precious seconds and allowed her facial bones to savor the hardness of his chest against her cheek, the feel of his shirt against her skin, and hear his heart beat, like a rhythmic drum that beat out his special cadence of support.

She'd never really been a girl to lean on people. Hadn't really learnt how until now. But she could lean on Levi. There was something magical about the way Levi could lift weariness from her like a blanket lifting from her shoulders. How he could energize her with a look let alone the circle of his arms.

She should have listened to him earlier when he wanted to explain. Shame she'd refused when she'd had the chance.

Her nose wrinkled. She could smell his blood. She focused on the damp patch a few inches from her nose and it was as if a beam of stark white light had been switched on in her brain. Her stupid brain that hadn't seen it all before while she'd been distracted by Odette's need.

How could she have missed it?

The bullet had been close. Could have hit his chest. Dead.

Like a splash of cold water from the river, the concept of Levi's death stared at her, shocking and far too real. It had been that dangerous.

He could have died. He could be dead now. No strong, vital heartbeat beneath her face.

The reality squeezed her lungs and her throat closed over. She'd been the greatest fool. She cared. Cared a lot. About Levi.

For the first time she realized how narrow her escape... from losing the man she suddenly couldn't doubt she wanted to know more. Why had it taken her so long to realize?

She wanted him.

The tears prickled then, and stung, and burned at the thought of Levi in mortal danger. She'd been obsessing about his perceived faults to protect her own realization. Of course she cared about him. What had she been thinking?

'So here we are again,' he said into her hair, and the vibration was all the more poignant for his mortality. Felt so much more precious than her own pride. If he'd been dead she'd have missed this. Any of this. All of this. Oblivious to her epiphany he went on musingly. 'I thought I'd seen the last of you.'

Thank God he hadn't. She closed her eyes and two fat tears ran down her cheeks. She swallowed and tried to level her voice. 'Fate conspires apparently.'

'Hmm.' He rumbled beneath her. 'Unfortunately, fate wasn't the only one conspiring. I'm sorry you and William are involved in this mess.'

Then she remembered she'd lied to him too and she hadn't told him. Suddenly it was so hard to start. Funny that. After all her bluster about being kept in the dark and her outrage at the misconceptions he'd practiced, she'd done the same.

'Congratulations on your nephew,' she said weakly as she pulled away. She turned to surreptitiously wipe her cheeks.

'Lucky baby to have a new beginning,' he went on dryly, and she could feel his eyes follow her as she widened the distance.

New beginnings. Could she do that? 'What would you do with a new beginning if you had one?' She took her eyes off the bank in front of them to look back at his face.

Maybe they could laugh about the irony.

She didn't see the grey crocodile move a foot closer to where they stood on the gravel. The whole world had condensed down to Levi, the fact she wanted to run back to his arms and didn't know if she could go through life denying that she'd the chance and blew it. About time she stopped lying to herself.

The huge crocodile stared with unblinking yellow eyes and opened his jaws.

Levi must have sensed or seen the sweep of the jagged tail out of the corner of his eye as the crocodile leapt because he caught Sophie's hand and pulled her back into his arms and towards the truck.

'Let's go. The crocs are getting hungry.'

She couldn't believe she'd forgotten the danger again. When she'd promised herself she wouldn't. Sophie twisted to look back and dread crawled when she saw how close to death they could have been.

Levi hugged her to him. 'My turn to warn you.'

His hand was tight around her wrist, painfully so, as he shuffled them both back towards the tree. Sophie glanced back. 'Too close,' she murmured with a shudder.

'Time to go, William,' he called over his shoulder and all Sophie could think about was the way her dog had died and the fact that she'd forgotten her own rules.

It could have attacked. She was the one who was supposed to know the dangers. When she leant up against the truck her legs trembled and threatened to collapse. They both could have been killed. She shuddered again and Levi must have sensed her jelly legs because he gathered her up and put her on the seat.

They both looked back and the crocodile had stopped in the spot they'd been standing. His thick reptilian tail swayed back and forth in frustration. His mate left the water and came to stand beside him.

Smiley whistled as he gathered the belongings and helped Odette move with her baby to the truck. 'We need to relocate those fellows,' Smiley said. 'Before they wipe your whole family out.'

'And yours,' said Levi grimly.

Smiley shook his head. 'Never seen 'em so nasty. It's not normal.'

'Spare me from feeling sorry for the crocodile.' Levi stared at the water. 'Though I wonder if that was planned, too? Steve could have been feeding them. Knowing Odette wanted to put a plaque up here.'

'If they don't catch him we'll never know.'

It was a subdued party that returned to Xanadu. Smiley drove, Odette and baby next to him and Levi and Sophie crammed into the long front seat like sardines in a tiny tin, with Odette's baby snuggled into Odette's chest.

Sophie sat on Levi and his arms held her as if he'd never let her go. Considering the day they'd had, well, Sophie was too tired to feel anything but comforted.

Levi ushered her into the resort building with his arm still protectively pulling her against him. Every now and then her mind recapped the morning, dwelling on Levi's close escape. 'I need to see your wound before we go.'

He frowned. 'It's nothing. We'll get Odette settled first and get you a stiff drink.' He signaled to one of the indoor staff.

She was over the crocodile. It was the shooting that rocked her. Levi could have died. 'Fine. But I'm not leaving until I've had a good look.'

He glanced at her as he waited to be put through to the police. 'Think about yourself for a change,' he said, and then he was issuing rapid fire instructions to whoever was on the other end of the line.

What about you? she thought, but didn't say it because there was so much she didn't know. But she watched the wound for more bleeding and if that happened all bets were off.

When he'd finished the call to the police – they'd apprehended the gunman, who was Steve, and he'd been placed in custody.

'I wish it hadn't been so,' he said to her, 'because now the breaking of the news to the staff becomes my next order of importance.'

She should be dressing his wound not watching Levi direct the world. 'Can't you do this later?' she asked with considerable exasperation.

He smiled down at her, and the way even that brief lift of his lips affected her heart was enough to warn her how bad it would be when he'd gone. 'What will you do when you don't have me to boss around?' he asked.

Not what she wanted to dwell on. 'Be lonely I guess.' She said it more to herself than to him. 'I'll find some first aid gear.'

'Wait, Sophie.' She began to move off and he caught her hand. Only this time her hand seemed to tangle in his as her fingers clasped his back.

He looked around at the milling staff and ushered her, not resisting for once, through the door and out onto the veranda and down the steps to the rustic bench under the massive boab.

He stared into her face and this time there was nowhere to hide. 'What did you mean? Be lonely, you guess?'

Could she do it? Throw it all away or be brave? The fear was there. The risk of pain greater than anything she'd experienced, but today's close shaves had taught her a valuable lesson. She had to take that risk or spend her life wondering.

'I'll be lonely without you.' She looked back at him. That strong jaw, that dangerous mouth, the man who'd stormed into her heart when she'd been kicking and screaming the whole way and he'd achieved it so easily in such a short time. 'I must have become used to having you around. In a week.'

She laughed mirthlessly at such foolishness. It was too late to deny a recognition on a different level. One between the two of them. This man had something in him that called to her the way no other person did.

She saw the trappings of wealth she'd said she despised and the evader of truth when she'd promised she'd never listen to another lie. But he hadn't been lying – her useless excuse to prevent falling for him - he'd been protecting her. Now she could see this man could be something very special in her life if she let him. And if he'd wanted to be.

Levi instinctively knew when she needed support and gave unstintingly from his own strength.

No one had ever understood her before.

That was the crux.

Levi got her. Knew where she was coming from almost before she did. 'Why is that?'

'Why is what?' he asked and she realized she must have spoken out loud.

'Why do you seem to understand me when others don't?'

His voice softened. 'If you tried, you could understand me too.'

When she looked into his eyes, past the clever knowledge in his, she saw him clearly, as if through a fresh pane of glass, unmarked by what had happened in the past. His caring, his readiness to learn new things, to listen to her point of view. His willingness to be there when the burden became too much for her, his hand there to pull her up and his arms ready to comfort.

Maybe she did understand him in ways she'd never wanted to understand others. And finally, with tiny tentative steps, she allowed herself to glimpse what life with Levi could be like. If she allowed herself to believe in him.

Was it that easy? 'Maybe I understand you a little.'

He slipped his good arm around her. 'Two people, from opposite ends of a huge country, meet and share extraordinary events. We've both changed, shared things, perhaps it's meant to be.'

She shook her head. It was all so confusing. 'How can it be, when you live somewhere I could never live?'

He smiled. 'And vice versa.'

Hopeless case. She'd known it. 'See?'

'We will. In time.' He hugged her and stood to help her up. 'Come on. You need to rest after all this excitement. It's been a big day.' He touched her cheek. 'But we're not finished with this subject.'

Then she remembered. If she was going to be brave she may as well finish it. 'And there's something I have to tell you.'

He stopped. 'Really?' He searched her face. Frowned, and then slowly, he smiled. 'Do I detect a hint of guilt?'

She blushed and muttered, 'Nothing wrong with your vision.'

And he laughed. His eyes opened wide with amusement. 'From Miss Trustworthy herself? Oh, this is too good.'

She didn't say anything and he pulled her back down on the seat. She tried to stand up again but he kept hold of her hand and she subsided.

'I'm not rushing this,' he said. 'This is priceless. Do go on.'

She ducked her chin, suddenly shy, then resolutely she raised it. 'You know when you asked if I knew the original family from Xanadu?'

'Hmm.'

Why did it feel as if he were watching her face more than listening to her words. 'Pay attention. I'm feeling bad here.'

He squeezed her shoulders. 'Good. You look hot when you're guilty.'

'I told you I didn't know.' She drew a deep breath, 'But I lied. I do know. It was my grandfather. Oh, and Smiley's grandfather. Our father's father.'

He laughed. 'You lied to me?'

She looked away. 'It was such a long story I didn't want to talk about it then.' How dare he laugh at her.

'You lied.'

She glared. 'Not as many times as you did but, okay, I admit there is a certain irony.'

'Brilliantly so.' He tilted his head and he wasn't smiling anymore. 'But I don't think I can talk to you right now. I'm too hurt that you deceived me.'

She frowned, frozen for a moment in time that she'd offended him deeply, before realizing he'd teased her. She glared at him. 'Surely not. Under all that moody exterior you're a comedian?'

'Moody... never. Workworn... yes.' He kissed her. 'And you have to admit. You not telling the truth is hilariously funny.'

She glared at him again but he'd moved on musingly. 'Smiley told me. Sullivan was his name. Your grandfather. I've already worked out you and Smiley should be the true owners of Xanadu?'

In another life. 'No.'

He tilted his head as he nodded. 'My grandfather cheated at cards and documented it. Was in fact very proud of scamming your grandfather out of his birth-right.'

Her foolish grandfather had lost it though. 'Nice genes you have, Dr Pearson.'

He winked at her. 'I'm working on that.'

What was that supposed to mean? 'Anyway, whatever he wrote, it's not legal.'

'Another of the things we'll discuss later.'

There was that money issue. She wished she could get over it. 'Are you very well off?'

He didn't smile but she could see the flicker of amusement at her prejudice. 'Afraid so. Stinking rich. Grandfather tripled the family coffers in his day and I've made some pretty useful investments too.'

'Oh.' He was so different to Brad. Nothing similar. She should have seen that earlier. 'You still work hard to help others though. When financially you don't need to do anything?'

'I need to for me. I'm not proud of my father or grandfather. Never a thought to benefit their fellow man. When my brother died I vowed I'd make him proud of me. Do some good.'

She savored the way he looked at her. As if she'd lightened his day just by being there. No one had looked at her like that since her parents had died. 'You seem so different from when you came.'

'Am I? Then you've made me so. I've been beating myself up for the last two years and had forgotten how to smile. A certain determined young midwife has made me realize there is more to life than regretting what can't be changed.'

'What couldn't be changed?' She needed to know. Needed to see what had formed this man she'd grown to love. To try, if she could, to help him. 'What hurt you? Tell me, Levi.'

'The loss of one of my patients. I blamed myself.'

'They died in an operation?'

'No, Miss Impatient. She didn't die in an operation. None of my patients have died in their operations.'

'Sorr-rry.' But she was glad. For his patients of course. But for him because she didn't want him hurt. It had come full circle.

She could see his regret. She reached out and caught his hand and held it in hers. 'Tell me.'

'Her name was Darla. She was twenty-three. The day I confirmed there was nothing I could do to restore her sight, she stepped in front of a truck.'

Oh God. Of course that would affect him. Sophie drew a sharp breath. 'Like your brother? Then it was probably an accident too,' she said earnestly. She saw the pain he still held and she squeezed his hand and her heart lifted when he squeezed back. She was glad to offer even that tiny comfort.

'Even if it was an accident,' he continued. 'It hit home and I blamed myself. Maybe there was something else I could have tried. Should I have encouraged more strongly her hope for the future of technology?' He shook his head over a tragedy that could never be rectified. 'It's too late for her but I doubled my workload. Tried to help more people until even my colleagues were telling me to take a break.'

She understood the concept of never doing enough. Had run herself ragged since returning to the Kimberley but for a different reason. 'You can't help the whole world.'

'When my father died suddenly, things in his will puzzled me. Leaving me Xanadu when it was supposed to go to Odette. I'd thought he hated me. I regretted I'd never tried to sway him towards a more fulfilling life. Behaved grown-up enough to talk to him, perhaps.'

Sophie squeezed the hand holding hers. 'People die and we regret what we didn't say. We all do.' One thing she didn't understand. 'But your father died five months ago. Why so long before you came here?'

He shrugged. 'I had to clear the backlog of cases I'd promised. And wait for the wet season to finish.' His gaze brushed over her and the glow in his eyes when he did so made her blush. 'I wish I'd come earlier.'

Imagine that. She'd have been in Perth and missed knowing him. Even if he broke her heart now, she could never regret that she'd met him. Had grown from knowing him in ways she'd never believe. 'Then lucky you didn't because I wouldn't have been here.'

He smiled down at her. 'Fate.'

'Serendipitous.' She snuggled under his arm, reluctant for this camaraderie to end. She'd learnt so much that helped her understand.

'Sophie.' He spoke into her hair.

She sighed. Soaking the moment in case it was the last time. 'What?'

'Look at me.'

He lifted his arm and she sat back and turned to face him. Her eyes met his and what she saw in them made the breath jam in her throat.

He lifted her hand and kissed her wrist. 'I see in you all the good things I wanted to find in myself. Things I find precious and uplifting and make me want to be a better man.'

She shook her head. She hadn't done anything.

Then he took both her hands in his and squeezed her fingers. 'I've come to know you... and to love you.' Her breath caught in her throat but he went on. 'I can't imagine going home without you. I can't imagine anywhere without you.'

She searched his face, not believing his words, but unable to stop the sudden gallop in her chest. He couldn't love her? She looked again and this time became a little less unconvinced as she saw the confirmation in his eyes. 'What are you saying?'

He smiled down at her. Like he really did love her? She hugged that impossible thought tightly as hope began to build. 'Will you marry me? Be my partner for life.' He lifted her hand to his mouth and kissed her palm, then folded her fingers over his salute. 'Can you love me back?'

She reached up and stroked his face. Those strong lines of cheek and jaw with the first regrowth of dark whiskers bristly beneath her fingers. How had she found him? Been so fortunate?

Her eyes stung and she chewed her lip, suddenly too frightened to say the words out loud. She took a deep breath and then she did.

'I already love you. Too much. Apparently since the waterhole on our trek. The moment you reached down to lift me. And then you kissed me and nothing was the same again.' She remembered the instant. 'I was so frightened you'd hurt me again I wasn't game to let the feeling out. And now you've exposed me.' Her eyes filled. 'So yes, please. If you promise not to lie to me, I will be your wife.'

'Never again.' Levi looked down at her. 'You'll keep me on the straight and narrow?' He gestured to the gorge below them. 'Even away from your beloved Kimberley?'

She shrugged. Suddenly home wasn't home if Levi wasn't there. 'We can visit.'

He pulled her close and held her against his heart as the world receded. Levi. Her heart. Her love. The other stuff they'd work out.

Chapter 12

Sophie gazed around at the guests at their wedding, an unlikely mix of smiling faces as the setting sun dusted the rugged ranges a glowing, loving lilac.

Loving like the vows she and Levi had exchanged above the stunning gorge at Xanadu and glowing like the look in her new husband's eyes.

She smiled at her friends – the sun-frocked women and their sun-browned men decked out in their best Akubra hats and polished boots – and Levi's friends in the sprinkling of suits and designer dresses, and the way the two groups melded with much gaiety under the leafless branches of the giant boab.

A tree that had grown more bulbous over the thousand years it had stood under a blue Kimberley sky and watched each turn of fortune this grand old homestead had seen since it was built by her great-grandfather and lost for two generations. Now hers and Levi's children, and maybe Smiley and Odette's children, would visit and one day those growing children would learn to love their heritage.

The cries of sulfur-crested cockatoos filled the late afternoon air and she lifted her head to allow the noise to soak into her memory as she inhaled the delicate aroma of the frangipani called Kimberley Gold in her bouquet. The heady scent enveloped the wedding party with purity fashioned by nature.

She'd be fine in the city. Beside her stood Levi, her husband, so tall and straight and gazing down at her with such a look of pride and love in his dark blue eyes. The tears pricked behind the mascara that Odette had insisted she wear, and she had to force her fingers not to rub her eyes.

He must have seen the glitter she tried to hide because his thumb gently rubbed hers in comfort. Already he knew what she was thinking, and magically the tears receded as his fingers entwined through hers. He looked down at the impressive pink Kimberley diamond ring they'd chosen from the mine, and she tutted as she followed his gaze. 'You have too much money.'

He smiled. 'Would you like me to give it all away?' The words were spoken lightly, but the look in his eyes assured her he was deadly serious and her heart thumped at the lengths this man would go to make her happy.

She blinked back more tears, refusing to weep even tears of joy on her wedding day. 'I could help you,' she smiled up at him, 'There's lots of things I'd like to improve around here.'

Even if I'm not here to see them, she thought, with barely any regret.

He hugged her to him. 'I can see I've taken on an expensive wife.' She felt his arm around her, so strong and sure of their love, and the truth was there to see. This was home. In Levi's arms. Not Xanadu, not busy Sydney, or wherever his work took him. Anywhere was home as long as she had Levi by her side.

The small plane – Levi had declined the helicopter with a smiling glance at his new wife – flew out the next morning, and with his hand in hers Sophie watched the brown earth pass beneath her with no regrets. The timeless mountains and steep-sided gorges would be there forever. Xanadu would stand watch over the land until she returned.

Now she could look to the future and new adventures with the man she trusted with all her heart.

That night in Sydney they dined at an exclusive restaurant overlooking Sydney Harbour, and Sophie could see why Levi loved it.

'This used to be my favorite place to eat,' Levi said as he gazed around at the panoramic harbor views and then back at his wife. Then he looked down at his plate and somehow she knew he was thinking of their bush-tucker hike through the hot bush. 'You've broadened my palate.'

'Do they serve grubs here?' she teased and stretched her hand out across the fine white tablecloth to his.

A frisson of magic passed between them and curved her lips in that persistent secret smile she'd had since last night. How could she not have known what had awaited her in Levi's arms? Yet what could have prepared her for the experience Levi had created as he'd shown her the meaning of giving and taking what love had to offer. Still her skin tingled and quivered as even a fleeting touch like this brought back memories and sensations she'd never imagined and their rings glinted as their fingers entwined.

His eyes smoldered and she felt her belly kick. 'You're blushing, my wife,' he teased.

Sophie fanned herself. 'Must be the food.'

'Strange, how the food is the last thing I'm thinking of. For you I would even eat a witchetty grub.'

Thank goodness this restaurant was discreet, but she needed to change the subject before her wicked husband said something even more outrageous. Sophie poked at the delicacies he'd ordered for her. 'I won't ask you if you don't make me eat that oyster.'

He laughed and took the morsel from her plate. 'I've something better for you.' She frowned as he reached into the pocket of his suit and withdrew a long white envelope.

Thick and embossed, he placed it in her hand with such an air of expectation she frowned.

'To my darling wife with love.' For a fleeting moment the weight of the paper sent an echo of mistrust and dread left from her dealings with Brad, but she banished it easily with her unswerving knowledge of Levi's love. Now what had he thought up?

She frowned down at the envelope and then back at him. 'What is this?' She weighed it in her hand and the thickness of paper folded had her intrigued.

'Open it.'

She tried, but it was sealed and stubborn, and Levi smiled as he handed her a knife to slit the edge. She glanced across at him.

Whatever it was he was enjoying this.

Finally the envelope opened and she eased the thick wad of paper out and unfolded it. It couldn't be... Her eyes widened as she moistened suddenly dry lips.

'A million acres?' She looked at him again and his blue eyes danced with amusement and love. 'You can't give me a million acres for a wedding present.'

He sat back to enjoy the view more. 'Why not?'

'It's too much.' She looked up at him. Not sure how he'd take the next thought. 'I'd want to give Smiley half.'

He grinned. Well pleased with himself. 'I thought you'd say that but he's agreed to be bought out.'

She frowned. 'Xanadu needs managing. We're living in Sydney.'

He raised his brows. 'Perhaps we should only live in Sydney six months of the year.'

He was enjoying this. Stringing her along. But she couldn't help the excitement that grew with each tumbled thought. 'And where will we be the rest of the time?'

'Guess?' He lifted her hand and ran his fingers along the soft skin before gently, and so reverently that her face flamed, he kissed her wrist. 'Let's spend that money you said I should give away.'

'By buying out Smiley?'

He shook his head and kissed her again and she watched the goose-flesh rise on her arms. She wished he wouldn't do that now because concentration was hard and she wanted to understand.

'By buying an outback eye clinic. The Sophie Pearson Mobile Eye Clinic, in fact.' He smiled. 'You'll be pleased to know it's made quite a dent in our wealth.'

She shook her head, overwhelmed by his vision, but he hadn't finished. 'I thought, if you agree, we'd travel north and visit outflung camps and missions during the dry, from May till October, and work together.'

She saw the passion in his eyes. The chance to do good work and she felt the tears well at her own fortune in finding a man she could be so proud of. She tilted her head and she'd bet there was the same excitement shining from her own eyes that she could see in his.

'Of course we'll need a base to work from and Xanadu fits the bill perfectly.'

She struggled to hold back her tears as she tried to take in the vision he'd created. 'Funny that.'

'And should you become otherwise engaged—' he glanced wickedly down at her narrow waist '—I can hire an assistant while you wait at home with our family. At Xanadu.'

He'd done this for her. 'You've thought of everything.'

His eyes darkened and she blushed right down to her toes and in all the places he'd discovered last night. 'And if we have children they will grow to love both homes.'

The warmth he created just by looking at her expanded until she could feel herself glow. 'You really have thought of everything.'

'I just follow the rule.' He leaned across and kissed her lips. 'Always tell the truth. And the truth is I will love my darling wife forever and ever.